THE KINGOWAN AFFAIR

THE KINGOWAN AFFAIR

Gillian Kaye

Chivers Press • G.K. Hall & Co.
Bath, England   Thorndike, Maine USA

This Large Print edition is published by Chivers Press, England, and by G.K. Hall & Co., USA.

Published in 2000 in the U.K. by arrangement with the author.

Published in 2000 in the U.S. by arrangement with Jill Kelbrick.

U.K. Hardcover   ISBN 0-7540-4202-4   (Chivers Large Print)
U.K. Softcover   ISBN 0-7540-4203-0   (Camden Large Print)
U.S. Softcover   ISBN 0-7838-9094-X   (Nightingale Series Edition)

The text of this Large Print edition is unabridged.
Other aspects of the book may vary from the original edition.

Set in 16 pt. New Times Roman.

Printed in Great Britain on acid-free paper.

British Library Cataloguing in Publication Data available

Library of Congress Cataloging-in-Publication Data

Kaye, Gillian.
   The Kingowan affair / Gillian Kaye.
      p. cm.—(Nightingale series)
   ISBN 0-7838-9094-X (lg. print : sc : alk. paper)
   1. Antique dealers—Fiction. 2. Divorced women—Fiction.
   I. Title. II. Series.
PR6061.A943 K56   2000
823'.914—dc21

00–039534

CHAPTER ONE

Jennie Graham heard the shrill ring of the doorbell and cursed quietly under her breath. She was tired after a long day at work and had been looking forward to a relaxing soak in the bath as soon as she had got home and before she had to prepare dinner for Stuart.

As she hurried downstairs to the front door, she wondered who could be calling at this hour. It was nearly seven o'clock in the evening and already getting dark. In early March, the light, spring evenings had still to come.

Through the coloured glass of the Victorian front door, she could see that the person standing there was quite tall. She opened the door rather impatiently, expecting yet another salesman for replacement windows or patio doors.

When she saw it was Amanda, she was pleased and then puzzled.

'Amanda, nice to see you, come in. Stuart isn't home yet.'

'I know he isn't.'

The short statement spoken in a tense, rather staccato tone gave Jennie a shock. Amanda was Stuart's partner and had always been friendly towards her.

As Jennie followed Amanda into the living-room, a sudden kaleidoscope of the last two years flashed across her mind. Meeting Stuart when she came to work in Edinburgh; falling in love with him after their first outing together and then marrying him two months later; setting up home in the large, Victorian, terrace house which he owned in a fashionable area, a year of happy marriage while she continued her job as secretary at an auctioneers' while Stuart developed his successful computer, printing business.

There followed another year which had been more successful, but less happy. Stuart had taken on Amanda Henderson as his partner and Jennie, liking Amanda immediately, had hoped that Stuart would be less busy and that she would see more of him. But her hopes were soon dashed as Stuart became preoccupied with his work and spent less and less time time at home.

When he was at home, he was tired and uncaring and in recent months, Jennie had forced herself to face up to the fact that their marriage was going through a difficult period. Now, as she put on the lamps in the living-room and drew the curtains, she wondered if she would dare to ask Amanda's advice. After all, Amanda was seeing more of Stuart than she was herself!

Amanda was all businesswoman, tall and always attractively dressed, with corn-coloured hair and brown eyes always with a glow of intelligence, sometimes a hint of hardness.

Jennie admired her while at the same time being unable to stop a sense of inferiority when she compared herself to her husband's partner. She had no idea that her own long, auburn hair and deep green eyes gave her a natural loveliness that the older woman did not possess, in spite of her striking looks.

'Jennie.' Amanda's voice broke into her thoughts. 'I've come to talk to you about Stuart.'

The voice was forthright and gave Jennie a momentary sense of confidence. Perhaps Amanda had been finding Stuart difficult, too, she thought.

'I'd be glad to talk to you, Amanda, though it doesn't seem right talking about Stuart behind his back. Is he still at the office?'

'Yes, but he knows I am coming to see you.'

'He knows?'

Jennie was bewildered and it sounded in her voice.

'Yes. We decided that it would be better if I spoke to you about the situation.'

We decided? The situation? Something must have gone wrong with the business, Jennie said to herself, but why couldn't Stuart have told her about it? Then she remembered the withdrawn Stuart of the past months and knew that their relationship had not invited confidences.

'I'm sorry that things aren't going well with

the business,' Jennie started to say, then she looked at Amanda's face and found herself unable to describe the expression in the dark eyes. They were almost scornful. 'I thought Stuart must have been worrying. He has been working so late, and week-ends, too, but he would never say anything about it to me and I didn't want to seem interfering. But it hasn't been easy. Perhaps it hasn't been easy for you either, Amanda.'

The other girl was silent and Jennie had an uneasy feeling that the expression on her face had turned to pity.

'Hasn't it ever occurred to you, Jennie, that Stuart might not have been very happy with you?'

Jennie's head shot up at Amanda's sharp-edged words, words implying a meaning that Jennie could not begin to guess at.

'Happy?' she floundered. 'Of course he's happy. I know he's been very tired with work, as though he'd had a lot on his mind, but we've only been married two years and . . .'

But a sharp and accusing interruption came forcefully from Amanda.

'In those two years, you can't have got to know Stuart very well if you think he's happy with you.'

Jennie stared in astonished bewilderment. 'But whatever . . . what do you mean, Amanda?'

'Haven't you noticed a change in him?

4

Didn't you ever think that he might be seeing someone else when he was out so late?'

Jennie stared again. 'Seeing someone else? You mean another woman?' She knew she sounded stupid.

Amanda laughed harshly. 'Yes, another woman. Good heavens, Jennie, couldn't you tell? Didn't you have any suspicions?'

Jennie shook her head. Suddenly, things were not making sense.

'Stuart loved me,' she said. 'And then . . . well, when our marriage seemed to be going wrong, I just thought it was because he was so tied up at work. He wouldn't have wanted anyone else, I'm sure he wouldn't, not if he had me.'

'Oh, Jennie, stop playing the innocent. You must know more about the world than that. Stuart stops taking an interest in you, so the first thing you think of has to be there must be someone else.'

Jennie got up and stood over Amanda and started to shout.

'I didn't think that! Why should I? Why should you even suggest such a thing?'

Amanda sighed. 'For goodness' sake, sit down. Now I know why Stuart wanted me to speak to you. I can't believe that you can be so trusting and innocent. Didn't you notice the difference after I joined the business? Didn't he start coming home less often? Didn't you wonder where he was?' Amanda's voice was

5

filled with cold sarcasm.

Jennie was sitting in stunned silence, listening to Amanda with a sense of disbelief, unable to say a word.

Amanda continued. 'No, I can see you trust him. I should have believed what he told me to expect. He's left it to me to tell you that ever since I came to the firm, he's been unfaithful to you. When he was late at work, he was with me. If he had to work at the week-ends, he was at my flat. We fell in love straight away. Stuart wants you to divorce him, so that he is free to marry me.'

Amanda's words seem to reach Jennie from a long way off. She felt a faint, swimming feeling in her head, a sickness in her stomach.

Stuart and Amanda? It couldn't be true, but when she looked at the radiant, good looks of the woman opposite her and then remembered how Stuart had changed in the last year, suddenly, she could believe it and with that belief came a surging anger.

'The brute. How could he! And not even having the courage to tell me himself. He makes you come and tell me the truth. All I can say, Amanda Henderson, is that you're welcome to him. You'll certainly not be able to trust him. And you can tell him from me that I never wish to set eyes on him again. This is his house and he's welcome to it. It had probably been someone else's cosy, little love-nest before I moved in. Tell him that I shall take everything that belongs to me and that I shall be gone by the end of the week. How could I have been so stupid not to see what was happening?'

'But, Jennie . . .'

'Don't "but, Jennie" me. He can move in with you until I'm gone and then this will be your home. Yes, he can have his divorce. I don't know how long it takes, but if he's already living with you, it shouldn't be difficult. Well, don't just sit there, Amanda! You've done his duty for him, so go back and tell him. You can find your own way to the door.'

'I'm sorry, Jennie.'

'Please go.'

Jennie heard Amanda make her way out of the living-room followed by the slam of the front door. Then she sat in her chair shivering, staring across the room, not seeing a thing. She could still hear Amanda's voice, remembering each word vividly.

I'm not going to cry, she said to herself, and with that thought, she got up and threw herself on to the settee and sobbed and cried as she had never cried before in her life.

Stuart, she cried his name aloud, I know you loved me to begin with. It was perfect. What a fool I was not to see it happening, but I trusted you. I don't think I shall ever trust a man again, never love again. Jennie repeated all these things to herself until she was exhausted, then she made herself get up and go into the kitchen and make herself some strong coffee. She couldn't eat, not now.

She wandered around the house, putting on all the lights and drawing the curtains. She looked at the pieces of furniture she had come to love because they had been Stuart's choice and he had good taste.

A lot of them were antiques; the Georgian, walnut chest inlaid with satinwood that was in the entrance was one of her favourites; her own books filled the glass-fronted bookcase; then there was the porcelain and china from Stuart's family that was kept locked away in the cabinet in the dining-room. None of it was hers; even the pictures on the walls had been bought by Stuart. She had her clothes, her books, her tapes, a few odd ornaments and some kitchenware she had brought from her own flat.

When she reached their bedroom, she cried again and then remembered that she had told Amanda that she would be out by the end of the week. What a foolish, hot-headed thing to say on the spur of the moment, she thought now, but to run away from it all had seemed the obvious thing to do.

She knew she had lost Stuart a long time ago and at that moment, she felt that it was not worth putting up a fight for someone who could behave as he had done. There was no time to feel sorry for herself, as it was now up to her to be sensible and to decide what to do with her life,

By eleven o'clock, she couldn't sleep and suddenly felt hungry. Perhaps the shock is wearing off, she said to herself. I'll have a bath and make a meal, try and think things out.

By the time she had cooked an omelette and made a salad, eaten it along with a glass of wine, she had a peculiar feeling of relief. She sat in the living-room with another cup of coffee and tried to work out her feelings.

I ought to feel heart-broken, she said to herself, but I don't. The most important thing seems to be that I won't have to go on living with a Stuart who is unpredictable and taciturn. All the tensions of the last year are over. I've got to come to a quick decision about where I'm going to live. And the sooner I do that, the sooner I can pick up the threads of a new life and try to forget about Stuart.

Jennie had been born and had grown up in the little town of Kingowan, not far from Loch Torvie. She was the eldest of the three McLeod children, her sister, Katrina, and her brother Angus still being at school. Her father kept a fishing accessories' shop and her mother was receptionist at the doctor's surgery.

The family lived happily and modestly in a small, stone house not far from the river and Jennie had grown up to fields and water and the not far-distant hills. When she was sixteen, she had decided to stay on at school and go

9

into the sixth form, but at the end of two years of study, she chose to travel each day to a secretarial college in the nearby town rather than go away to university.

On her eighteenth birthday, her father had given her a second-hand car to travel back and forth and when, two years later, she had met Stuart and had just married, they had sold the little car and Stuart had bought her a larger, newer one. Now twenty-two, she knew that she was going to find the car very useful in moving her stuff out of the house.

It didn't take Jennie long in deciding to go back to Kingowan. Although she had enjoyed her years in Edinburgh, there was much about life in a small, country town that she missed and she knew that her mother would welcome her at home until she decided on her next step.

In the end, she slept well for what was left of the night and awoke next morning to find herself in a positive mood and with a determination not to let Stuart Graham ruin her life.

Later that morning, at the Edinburgh auctioneers where she had worked for three years, she saw one of the partners, Donald Grant, and explained her position to him.

'I am very sorry, Jennie, to hear your news. I am sure you deserved better than that.' She had always got on well with him and his tone was kindly. 'Does it mean that we are going to lose you?'

'I have to give you a week's notice, Mr Grant,' she replied. 'But I have some holidays left so I wondered if you would let me leave at the end of the week. I've decided to go back to Kingowan for the time being.'

'So you want to be off on Friday. Well, come and see me before you go and I'll give you a reference. It will be hard to replace you, Jennie.' He shook her by the hand. 'Let me know if there is anything I can do.'

The worst thing about the rest of that week was Jennie's dread that she would have to see Stuart. She knew that as long as she was on her own and kept herself busy, she would remain composed, but she wasn't sure of her reaction if she had to meet him face to face.

In the end, there was so much to do that Friday was with her almost before she had got used to the idea that she was going to leave Edinburgh. She had phoned Stuart's secretary and left a message to say that she was leaving the house, had taken all her possessions and that she would put the keys through the letter-box.

She had also spoken to her mother. Mrs McLeod had been upset initially, but then pleased that Jennie wanted to come home though she did warn her daughter that she would have to share a bedroom with her sister, Katrina.

*   *   *

It was lovely to be back in Kingowan, the river so near, with lovely walks in the spring afternoons and the hills blue-grey in the distance. The small town seemed so friendly and welcoming. Jennie had decided to take a week off before she started to look for a job.

She knew it was not going to be easy to find one in Kingowan and she knew she might have to go farther afield. She was thankful she still had her car.

At the end of that first week, Mrs McLeod, going upstairs one evening, found Jennie in tears in the bedroom her two daughters were sharing.

'Why, Jennie, lass, whatever is it? Has it all suddenly come over you?'

Jennie threw herself into her mother's arms.

'Oh, Mum, have I done the right thing? It's lovely being back at home in Kingowan, but I can't get used to sharing with Katrina. She's so untidy and she plays her music so loud.'

She looked up as her mother burst out laughing.

'Whatever is there to laugh at?' she asked indignantly.

'Oh, I'm sorry, Jennie. I know it's not funny to you, but when you were sixteen and the same age as Katrina is now, it was one long battle to get you to keep the room tidy and to stop you playing your records loud so that they didn't upset Dad.' She gave Jennie a hug. 'I shouldn't have laughed at you. It's not easy, is it?'

Jennie sighed. 'No, it isn't. At first, I was so furious with Stuart I was glad to let him go, but now I seem to miss him so much. And it's not fair on Katrina either to have to share with me, and she and Angus always seem to be quarreling about something. I just can't help wishing there was somewhere I could be quiet.'

She noticed the concern on her mother's face. 'I'm the one who should be saying sorry, Mum. You've been so good to let me come home and now I seem to be grumbling.'

'I understand, Jennie. You're older than the other two and used to having a place of your own. But what is the answer? Can you afford to take a flat somewhere?'

Jennie was thoughtful. 'I think I could if I got a good enough job. I shall have an allowance from Stuart, after all. Somehow there was something in me that wanted to return to Kingowan. I just felt as though I could cope if I was back here.'

'You'll have to get the Perth paper next week and see if there are any jobs advertised. You've got good qualifications and a lot of useful experience. You shouldn't find it too difficult to get a good job.'

Jennie smiled. 'Sensible Mum. It's early days, isn't it? And I'll just have to try and keep out of Katrina's way.'

Later in the evening, Mrs McLeod came

13

looking for Jennie, a newspaper in her hand.

'Jennie, listen to this. It's in the free, local paper that's just been delivered.'

Jennie looked up with interest. 'You sound quite excited,' she said.

Mrs McLeod started to read out loud. 'Assistant wanted for small, antique shop, some experience of antiques required. Small flat for single person available above shop. Applications with names of referees to Adrian Challis at Kingowan Antiques.'

Jennie frowned as she listened and as she looked at her mother, her expression was hesitant. 'But, Mum, I've never worked in a shop. I've no experience of selling at all. I must admit it sounds good but I don't think I'd stand a chance.'

Her mother was thrusting the paper into her hand. 'You read it. You've been working with antiques all the time you've been at the sale-rooms. That's bound to count for something, and the flat, Jennie. I haven't been into it, but it's in a nice position. You know where it is, don't you?'

'Yes, it's down Crieff Road, opposite the bookshop. I've been in the bookshop often, though I don't like the owner. He's always so superior . . .'

'Jennie, never mind the bookshop. You've got to take it seriously if you want to stay in Kingowan. This seemed like a heaven-sent opportunity.'

14

Jennie was looking closely at the advertisement and as she read it again, she felt a slight raising of her spirits. It was true she did know something about antiques. You couldn't be secretary to an auctioneer without learning a lot of what was going on. It should be easy enough to get used to the shop side of the business. Was her mother right?

'Who is this Adrian Challis, Mum? He's not a local man, is he?'

'No, I think he's from London, but he has several antique shops in Scotland. I know there's one in Pitlochry and Braemar, too, I believe.'

'I wonder who has been working there until now?'

Her mother seemed to know everything that was going on in Kingowan.

'That Mrs Cameron, the wife of the deputy-head at the High School has been there for a couple of years. But Mr Cameron has got a school of his own in Perth now. He starts next term, so I expect they're moving house. I think the flat above the shop has been empty.'

Jennie had been thinking while her mother had been speaking and had come to a decision.

'I think I will have a go,' she said. 'It couldn't have come at a better time and I've got nothing to lose if I don't get it. Thank you, Mum.'

By the next afternoon, Jennie had posted her application and had taken a walk down into the town to have a look for the shop. It was in a road which was a favourite tourist haunt, with several shops. There was more than one antique shop, the bookshop and various craft and gift shops.

Jennie passed Kingowan Antiques, but didn't go in. There were a few pieces of china and porcelain in the window and beyond that, she could see the mellow gleam of old furniture. She looked up and saw two, small windows which must belong to the flat. Suddenly, she felt excited. I would like it, she said to herself. I really do believe I would like living and working here.

The next few days were spent watching the post anxiously for a reply to her application. After a week, her spirits had sunk to zero. But, one afternoon, returning from a walk by the river, Jennie found her mother waiting for her.

'Jennie, is that you? Come quickly, to the kitchen. There's a telephone message for you. Mr Challis rang up half-an-hour ago. He asked if you would ring him back. The number's by the phone, a Perth number.'

Jennie picked up the telephone and dialled the number.

'Mrs Graham? Good. I'm interested in your application. Would you be good enough to come and see me at the shop tomorrow afternoon at two o'clock? You know where it is? Good. I will see you then. Goodbye.'

CHAPTER TWO

The next afternoon, Jennie dressed very carefully for her interview. They were now almost into April and the wintry weather of March seemed a thing of the past. On her way to Kingowan Antiques, she found herself speculating on the age and looks of Adrian Challis, trying to match him to the voice on the phone. When she reached Crieff Road, she was feeling as nervous as a schoolgirl going for her first job.

She opened the door of the shop and immediately liked the smell of the wax polish and old wood that greeted her. She had hardly had time to register the value of the pieces of furniture she saw about her, when a tall man stepped from the back of the shop.

At first sight, and mainly because his hair was dark and greying, she took him to be an older man, but as he came forward and shook her by the hand, she could see by his smile and from his voice that he would be in his late thirties. His looks were as attractive as his voice had sounded on the phone; even, handsome features on a slightly-lined face and lively, grey eyes with a warm look in them.

'Mrs Graham, I am pleased to meet you. Come and sit down and tell me about yourself. There's a small office at the back of the shop and we shall hear if any customers come in.'

Jennie followed him and found herself facing him across an old, leather-topped desk.

'I will be honest with you and tell you that I was particularly impressed by your experience with Moncrieff and Grant, in Edinburgh, and I have been on the phone to them. They have given you an excellent reference. It seems that they were sorry to lose you.'

His look was suddenly penetrating. 'How is it that you have left Edinburgh so suddenly to come and live in Kingowan? And why do you choose to apply for a job in a shop when you have such good secretarial qualifications?'

Jennie hadn't expected such personal questions and was unprepared for them. To her horror, she found herself stammering.

'I had to leave . . . you see my home is here . . . I was pleased because you were offering the flat above the shop.'

She stopped and drew in a deep breath.

'I'd better be honest with you. My husband and I have split up and I had no claim on the Edinburgh house we were living in. I was anxious to come back to Kingowan, where my parents still live. But I have younger brothers and sisters and staying there is not really convenient. That's why I was attracted by the job you offer, because of the flat. I desperately need somewhere to live. I have never worked in a shop, but I think I could do it.'

He didn't reply straight away but got up

18

from the desk and moved towards the door.

'Come into the shop with me.'

In the shop, Jennie looked around her and saw clearly for the first time that it was full of beautiful furniture, china and silver. Then, to her surprise, she realised Adrian Challis was questioning her quite sharply.

'Now, I want you to tell me what you know about anything you can see here. How much that chest is worth for example.' He pointed to a bow-fronted, Regency chest-of-drawers.

'It is Georgian,' she replied without hesitation. 'I should think it is worth about one thousand pounds.' She looked up at him. Was she making a fool of herself? 'It is mahogany, isn't it?'

He made no comment, but nodded and pointed to the plates arranged in racks along the wall.

'And that plate there? The second from the end.'

She frowned for a moment. 'The blue and white one? I think that's Lowestoft, but I'm not sure of the value. About eighty to one hundred pounds, I should think.'

Again he nodded and walked over to a solid chest standing near the door.

'And this?'

Jennie was more confident this time. 'Oh, it's earlier and it's an oak coffer, I should think about seventeenth century. The carving is lovely, isn't it?'

'And the price?'

She thought for a moment. 'One thousand pounds, perhaps more. I'm not too sure about that.'

She looked at him anxiously as he came up to her and put an arm round her shoulders.

'Full marks. You really do know it, and you love it, too, don't you?' he said.

'Yes, I do love it, but Mr Challis, I've never worked in a shop before.'

He was smiling. 'It doesn't matter, I can soon teach you about credit cards, cheques and banking, and things like that. When can you start?'

Jennie looked at him unbelievingly. 'Do you mean I've got the job?'

'You have, Jennie. I'm going to call you Jennie and you must call me Adrian. I was so sure that I didn't even bother to arrange any other interviews. I only needed to see you and it didn't take long to confirm that I'd made the right choice. And now, you'll want to see the flat. That's important to you, isn't it? The stairs are at the back of the shop and you have a back door with your own key.'

Jennie followed him, her mind in a whirl. This was all too easy! There had to be some snag! But when she saw the flat, she fell in love with it. The building was low and old and the upstairs rooms were built into the roof space, each one with sloping ceilings and dark, oak beams.

There were three rooms, none of them big. The living-room overlooked the street, with the two, small windows she had seen from the outside. It was simply furnished, with two easy-chairs, a small dining-table and a bookcase. They walked along the landing to the bedroom which was also small with a single bed and a window which looked over the tops of Kingowan's houses to the river.

'Is there a kitchen?' Jennie asked. 'And a bathroom?'

He grinned. 'Nothing has been forgotten. Not much space but everything you need.'

He opened a door between the two rooms and she was delighted to find a shower unit and, farther along the small passage, an archway through to a small kitchen.

'There you are,' he said. 'There was no window in this space, so I put a skylight in the roof. It isn't difficult to open.'

He watched as she looked around the kitchen, a pleased look on her face.

'Well, will it suit you?' he asked.

She turned towards him and smiled. 'It is lovely. It really couldn't be nicer and I'd be very pleased to accept the job, if you are sure.'

'I am sure, but shall we say a month's trial on both sides? Let's go back to the office now and we'll sort out salary and holidays and things like that. I hope you won't mind working on a Saturday, but I close the shop all day Monday. Oh, and we don't have an early-

21

closing day.'

In the office, he produced a contract which Jennie signed. The salary was good and the rent for the flat was very reasonable. He had explained that there was a parking space in the lane at the rear of the property if she had a car. There was no garden, just a yard which had a clothes' line and a few shrubs in stone tubs.

'When do you want me to start?' Jennie asked, wondering if he was going to throw her in at the deep end and leave her to work things out for herself or whether Mrs Cameron would be there to show her the running of the shop.

'Can you start on Monday?'

She looked at him. 'Monday? The day after tomorrow?'

'Yes, you see Mrs Cameron left yesterday and I am going to be here for a few days. If you can come in on Monday, I'll be able to show you how I like things managed. You can move into the flat tomorrow if you like. I'll give you the keys and explain the burglar alarm. I'm living in Perth, so I can meet you here at about ten o'clock on Monday morning. It's our day for closing so it will be a good chance to explain everything to you. Does that suit?'

She nodded. 'Yes, thank you, that would suit me fine.'

'And, Jennie, I hope you won't mind me mentioning this. You are dressed very nicely today. You look lovely in fact, and I do expect a good standard of dress from my staff. No jeans and trainers, if you don't mind.'

'It's all right.' She laughed. 'I had to wear skirts and blouses at Moncrieff and Grant, so I won't let you down, I promise.'

As she left the shop, she decided she liked Adrian Challis. To begin with, with his good looks and his easy flattery, she had taken him to be a charmer, but by the end of the interview she had to acknowledge his keen, business-like manner and his obvious enthusiasm for his work. It looks as though I have fallen on my feet, she thought, as she walked home to tell her mother the good news.

The next day, with Katrina's help, she spent the whole morning moving her belongings into the flat. She put on the fires to warm it through. By four o'clock, she made her last journey, put the last of her belongings in place, then she and her mother went for a cup of tea.

In Jennie's first two weeks, Adrian spent quite a lot of time with her and she soon learned that he would visit the shop in Kingowan once a week to bring in pieces of furniture if she had made sales and to make sure that she had plenty of porcelain and smaller items.

She discovered that his main shop was in Perth and that he also had a house there. He'd said nothing about a wife and family and she hadn't liked to ask him if he was married or not.

By her second day, she had decided that she liked Adrian Challis very much. After the parting with Stuart, she had thought that she would be apprehensive and distrustful about other men, but Adrian was so open and friendly that her fears were soon dispelled.

He usually arrived about ten o'clock and before that, Jennie made sure that she had been round the whole shop and dusted everything. The job made her smile rather ruefully for she had always hated housework and suddenly she found herself liking the task and handled each piece of china and each article of furniture with great care.

She was sitting with Adrian in the office going through some paper work when the sound of the old-fashioned shop bell at the front door signalled a customer. She saw that it was an elderly gentleman, short and rather stout, with a shock of white hair. Before she had time to greet him, Adrian had come forward and was all smiles.

'Colonel Fairfax, I am so glad that you have come in as I would like to introduce you to Jennie. Mrs Cameron left last week.' He turned to Jennie. 'Colonel Fairfax is one of our best customers. I want you to take care of him.'

The colonel shook hands and his voice held a note of pleasure.

'I'm very pleased to meet you, young lady. May I call you Jennie? I come over from Glentorrah about once a week, but if Adrian has anything he knows I will like, he'll ask you to give me a ring.'

'Colonel Fairfax has a particular interest in George the Third mahogany,' Adrian said. 'And he always keeps his eyes on the plate racks. Sometimes I think he knows more than I do about that period.'

Jennie looked from one to another and smiled. 'You are making me feel nervous,' she said.

'Now, Jennie, you know you are doing well.' Adrian turned to the other man. 'Jennie used to work with Moncrieff and Grant in Edinburgh. You'll know them well, colonel.'

'Yes. Many a fine piece I've bought in their sale room and not cheaply either!'

Jennie left the two men to chat and went back into the office. It looked as though she was going to have to get used to knowledgeable customers who knew Adrian well.

Half-an-hour before they were due to shut up that night, Adrian, who had been at a house sale a few miles away, arrived back in the shop carrying a heavy box.

'Not bad, Jennie, not bad. A few pieces of Minton, some Staffordshire figures and some nice glass. We'll leave it in the box and you can help me price it in the morning. It'll be good practice for you.' He was much taller than she was and stood looking down at her with an unfathomable expression in his eyes.

'What are you doing this evening, Jennie? I don't suppose you would let me take you out to dinner, would you?'

She looked up in surprise. She hadn't been expecting such an invitation and didn't quite know what to say.

He continued without seeming to need an answer. 'I expect you'll be having a meal on your own upstairs, so I thought perhaps we might go to the Ben Rachan Hotel, down on the loch. How about it?'

She still hesitated though she couldn't quite explain why.

'I'm not sure . . .' she stammered, feeling a blush creep into her cheeks.

He looked at her troubled face. 'Is it to do with your husband, Jennie? It's not easy, is it? But you can't stay on your own for ever and sometimes it's good to have someone to talk to. I'm a good listener.'

She looked into his eyes and liked the sincere, sympathetic expression. She made up her mind.

'Well, yes, Adrian, I think I would like it. I haven't been out anywhere since I came back to Kingowan.'

After the shop was closed, Adrian sent Jennie upstairs to change while he busied himself in the office. An hour later, they were driving towards Loch Torvie and Jennie felt a strange sense of exhilaration. He didn't speak and she was quiet, too. She loved this road and knew they would soon get their first glimpse of the water.

Then, suddenly, Adrian took a narrow turning off the road, taking them into a leafy drive leading to a gracious, square, stone building, once a country house. Lying at the foot of Ben Rachan, between hill and loch, its gardens ran right down to the waterside.

When Adrian had stopped the car, Jennie got out and looked about her. She had been born within miles of these shores yet she never failed to be entranced by the glittering, still water and the backcloth of hills that turned a misty blue as she looked down the loch.

Adrian locked the car and joined her.

'Have you been here before, Jennie?' he asked.

'No, I haven't. I know the loch well, but the hotel is new to me. I think it was a private house until a couple of years ago.'

'They usually have a very good menu. Shall we go and eat? We've hardly stopped all day and I'm hungry. We can walk along the loch afterwards.'

Jennie enjoyed the meal. The food was excellent and the atmosphere not too formal. Adrian was in what she was coming to recognise as one of his flattering moods, out to charm, but it amused her rather than annoyed her. She didn't drink a lot of wine, but as they walked across the gardens and down to the loch after the meal, she suddenly felt carefree. It was a feeling she had almost forgotten.

A footpath wound through the trees at the water's edge and as they walked along, Adrian was very close. Suddenly, she felt him take her hand. She glanced up quickly to find him smiling at her, a boyish grin and seeing it and his air of friendliness, Jennie let her hand remain in his grasp.

'You look different this evening, Jennie. I do believe it's the first time you've relaxed and enjoyed yourself for a long time. Am I right? Was he a rotter, that husband of yours?'

Jennie found that she didn't mind his questions and it surprised her, as she had known him only a few days, yet she felt she knew him well. There was something in his handsome, intelligent face that inspired confidence.

In recent months, she had never spoken to anyone about Stuart, not even to her mother. Suddenly, she felt that she could talk and that she wanted to, and Adrian turned out to be a very good listener. She stopped abruptly after several minutes, and a faint colour came into her cheeks.

'I'm sorry, Adrian. I don't know why I'm telling you all this. It must be the dinner and the wine.'

'And the company, I hope.'

She laughed. 'Yes. I suddenly felt I could talk to you. Now you know why I came back to Kingowan and needed a job and a home so urgently.'

'Your misfortune is my good fortune, Jennie. I hope you are going to like working at Kingowan Antiques.'

'I do already,' she said.

His hold on her hand tightened. 'I think you have a natural love of old and beautiful things. It's not surprising. You are very beautiful yourself.'

She snatched her hand away. 'No, Adrian, no flattery, please. I'm in no mood for it and I want to feel I can trust you. I didn't think I would trust anyone again after Stuart.'

'I'm sorry. I've no wish to upset you after such a pleasant evening. Let's walk up as far as those trees and then we'll turn back. I still have to drive home to Perth.'

She looked at him curiously and couldn't stop the next question.

'Aren't you married, Adrian?'

He gave a grin. 'Thirty-seven years old and still a bachelor! I never seem to meet the person I want to spend the rest of my life with. I'm too restless, I suppose, like to be on the move all the time.'

Jennie was glad that his reply had given her the chance to turn the conversation away from personal things.

'How many shops do you have?' she asked.

29

'Well, you know about the main one in Perth. I have a manager and an assistant there. You must meet Lorna one day. I think you would like her. The other shops are small places, like Kingowan, and two of them I only open in the tourist season. One of those is in Braemar and the other in Kingussie. There is one other in Pitlochry, where I have another manager, Tony. You must meet him, too. So you can see that between the shops and fitting in auctions and house sales I am kept very busy and wouldn't make a good husband!'

They walked back to the car and then drove back to Kingowan in a companionable silence. At the shop, Adrian went into the office to collect his briefcase. Jennie waited for him. At the door, he dropped a kiss on her cheek, no more than a brush of his lips.

'Thank you for a lovely evening, Jennie. We must do it again.'

She ignored the brief caress and walked with him out to the car. As he opened the door, a figure called to him from across the road and Jennie heard the exchange of greetings.

'Hello, Adrian. I haven't seen you for a long time. Everything all right?'

'Hello, Ian.' Then Adrian turned and called across the body of the car to Jennie. 'Jennie, have you met Ian? He owns the bookshop across the road, Kingowan Books. Ian McWilliam, meet Jennie Graham, my new assistant.'

The stranger had come over the road and stood towering above her. He was very tall, a young man of about thirty, with very dark hair and a serious, good-looking face with intelligent, grey eyes.

However, as Jennie looked up and recognised the bookseller, it was to meet a frowning gaze and a look of vague disapproval. His words were amiable enough, though, as he shook her hand and spoke in a deep, slow voice.

'I'm pleased to meet you, Jennie, though I fancy I have seen you in the bookshop in the past.'

'Yes, I used to come in before I moved to Edinburgh,' she replied. 'It was quite a long time ago.'

'Ian's a good friend, Jennie. If you need any help you only have to cross the road. I'll be on my way now. See you in the morning. One more day and then you'll be on your own. Goodbye, Ian. We must have a drink sometime.'

Ian McWilliam had crossed the road again without saying another word to Jennie. She waved goodbye to Adrian and went back into the shop to lock up and set the alarm.

The next morning, Adrian arrived at his usual time, not in his car, but driving a big, white van with his name in black printed neatly on each side.

Jennie helped him carry in a set of Victorian dining-chairs and then they unpacked his purchases from the house sale the previous day. She found it quite exciting to unwrap each piece of porcelain and glass and, after the pricing had been done, Adrian left to drive up to Braemar.

Jennie settled to cleaning the plates and glassware and displaying them in the shop. She had two customers in the afternoon, but neither of them bought anything. Not a very good start, she said to herself, looking up hopefully when she heard the shop bell ring, just on closing time.

The figure standing inside the door, however, was a familiar one and not a customer. It was Ian McWilliam. She walked across the shop to speak to him.

'Are you about to close?' he asked rather tersely.

Jennie stared at him, prepared to be friendly, but his tone was stiff.

'Yes. It's just coming up to six o'clock,' she replied.

He stood looking down at her as though he was trying to decide what to say. When his words came, they were short and abrupt.

'I don't want to interfere,' she heard him saying, 'but I thought I should warn you about Adrian Challis.'

CHAPTER THREE

Jennie continued to stare at the man standing in the doorway, wondering if she had heard him correctly.

'Warn me about Adrian?' she said almost shrilly. 'Whatever do you mean?'

Without saying anything else, he stepped into the shop.

'It's six o'clock,' she said sharply. 'I must lock up and set the alarm. I can't imagine what it is you want to say to me, or even if I want to hear it, but you'd better go into the office. I'll join you.'

He started to walk through the shop, leaving Jennie to set the alarm and follow him. She was still mystified and somewhat angry at his words. He didn't go through into the office but sat down on one of the dining-chairs that Adrian had brought in that morning. Jennie sat opposite him.

'Well, whatever it is you have come to say, I can't see that it is any business of yours what goes on when I am working here. Adrian has been good enough to give me the job and has been most helpful this week showing me how everything is managed.'

His expression did not change, but stayed as serious and grim as it had been when he came into the shop.

'Adrian may be a good businessman,' he said, 'but his reputation with women is notorious and I just didn't want to see a young girl like you taken in by him. I wanted to put you on your guard.'

Jennie felt herself getting hot with anger.

'Mr McWilliam . . .'

'Ian, please,' he interrupted.

'Mr McWilliam—I prefer to be formal. I resent your slurs against Adrian and I resent you calling me a young girl. I am twenty-four and have been married for two years. I am well able to take care of myself.'

His tone softened slightly. 'I always think of you as the young McLeod girl who used to come in for books. Time slips past so quickly.'

'You are trying to evade the issue. Why should I have to believe anything you have to say about Adrian?'

'Jennie, Adrian is a very charming and clever man. I have seen one young girl very hurt by his behaviour and I don't know why, but I suddenly felt I wanted to save you from the same experience.'

She looked at him; his dark, wavy hair worn slightly long, the serious and sensitive lines of his face, the intent look in his grey eyes. Suddenly, he seemed sincere and trustworthy, but she still felt annoyed at his interference and was defending the Adrian she had come to like.

'It sounds as though it was something in the

past, and I don't know that I want to listen to you.'

'It was last summer, and the girl was my assistant. She was with me a year before going to university. Adrian was intrigued with her, and took her everywhere. I should think he spent more time in Kingowan than in any of his other shops, and, of course, she fell for him and was all prepared not to go to university so that she could stay near him. I tried to persuade her but she wouldn't take any notice.'

Jennie interrupted rather rudely.

'What happened? How did it end?'

'It ended with a visit from Lorna, the manager of the Perth shop and the woman Adrian lives with, or at least spends most of his time with. She had found out about Fiona and came over to warn her off. They were in the back of my shop and when it was over, Lorna left. Fiona was hysterical, went home and took an overdose.'

'You mean . . . ?'

'No, she didn't die. Her parents got her to hospital in time. It turned out that she thought she was pregnant and that Adrian had promised to marry her. She was wrong, as it turned out, and her parents were sensible and took her away. She's settled down at university now, but I didn't want to see it happening all over again.'

Jennie looked at him and saw to her

surprise that he was genuinely concerned.

'You are telling me the truth, aren't you?'

'Yes.'

'Well, thank you, but it wasn't necessary. I am actually in the middle of divorce proceedings and have no intention of getting myself entangled with another man, certainly not with Adrian Challis.'

Ian McWilliam got up. 'I'm glad to hear it. I hope you'll forgive me saying what I did. I know it's no business of mine, but I felt I had to talk to you. I'll go now but you know where I am if you need any help. And, please, call me Ian.'

She smiled for the first time. 'I don't suppose I can go on calling you mister when your shop is just across the road. Thank you, Ian, and I am sorry I was angry at first. I thought you were being unnecessarily interfering.'

'I understand, Jennie. Goodbye.'

Jennie was thoughtful after Ian had gone. Life is never simple, she thought. I came to quiet Kingowan to get out of Stuart's way and immediately become involved with a womanising antique dealer and a scholarly bookseller. Then she grinned to herself. It will take my mind off Stuart, she thought. I don't think I shall have any trouble from Adrian Challis.

Time passed quickly and Jennie grew to love the shop. She got to know the regular customers, among them Colonel Fairfax, who came in once a week to see what Adrian had brought, but he did not always buy anything. Adrian came every Wednesday and sometimes stayed into the evening.

On these occasions, Jennie would give him supper in the flat or occasionally they would go out for a meal at the Ben Rachan Hotel. Adrian was always good company and did not attempt any romantic advances. Gradually, she forgot about Ian's warning.

During this time, she received her petition for divorce. Stuart was not contesting the petition. It was a strange, twilight time, married and yet not married and, incredibly, forgetting about Stuart very quickly.

As the summer approached and the evenings got warmer and longer, Adrian got into the habit of coming over to Kingowan on one of the evenings when she hadn't seen him during the day and they would take a leisurely walk along the river. It was on these occasions that warning bells started to ring for Jennie. She could tell he was attracted to her and she began to feel at ease in his company.

It was Adrian's custom to leave her at the front of the shop when they returned from their walk and she would then say goodbye and walk round to the back door of the flat while he got into the car and drove off.

On one of these occasions, a sudden shower had caught them unawares as they walked along the river bank. Laughing, they had run for shelter to the nearest trees and stood there, close together, watching the spatter of heavy rain on the water. His arm was around her shoulders and Jennie felt herself give a shiver at the delicate touch.

'Cold, Jennie?' His voice was casual and soft.

'No,' she replied, a little confused. 'I expect it's the rain.'

'Perhaps we had better make a run for it. We're not far from the shop and the rain doesn't look like stopping.'

She was glad of the suggestion and hoped it had dispelled the moment of the sensation of his touch. They kept under the trees along the path and didn't get a soaking until they were running along Crieff Road towards the shop. Adrian stopped when they reached his car, his shirt clinging to him now.

'Jennie, would you mind if I came in to dry off?' he asked.

'No, of course not. I'll put the heater on and get us some coffee.'

They hurried round to the back lane and by the time they had climbed the stairs, they were both out of breath and laughing.

'You'd better go and change your dress, Jennie. I'll put on the fire.'

She slipped quickly into another dress and returned to the living-room.

'You look beautiful, Jennie.'

'Adrian.' She said only his name, but her tone was sharp.

He laughed. 'You must let me say what is the truth. I've thought you were a beautiful girl from the beginning, but tonight, the rain and the run we had from the river seems to have given you an extra radiance.'

Jennie stopped in the doorway. She didn't want his compliments and she didn't like the look in his eyes. She felt suddenly foolish for having let him come back to the flat, and decided not to take any notice.

'I'll get some coffee,' she said but stopped as his voice called her name.

'Come here, Jennie.'

She met his eyes as his hand reached out and took her arm. He drew her towards him. He had slid his hands gently up her arms before she started to struggle away from him, but she was caught in a hard embrace, his mouth forcing down on hers. After that, she was lost, and she returned his kiss.

'You want me as much as I want you,' he whispered as they drew apart. 'Do you want me to stay?'

It was the smooth tones, the self-satisfied certainty that made Jennie see what was happening and made her speak swiftly and without really thinking.

'I'm not one of your girls for the taking, Adrian Challis. Just leave me alone and go. Go back to your girlfriend, and in future, it will be strictly business between us.'

'You little vixen, and I thought you'd be easy. But I shan't give up. You've got me interested now, Jennie Graham.'

'Business only, Adrian.' Her voice was cold.

'Business only it is, Jennie . . . for the time being. Goodbye. I'll be over with the van next week.'

And as she stood there, he left the room, hurried down the stairs and out of the back door.

Jennie smiled ruefully. 'I must be the most trusting fool on this earth,' she said out loud, and then she thought of how Ian had warned her and how angry she had been with him and quick to spring to Adrian's defence. I wonder if I'll ever love anyone again, she thought. Perhaps Stuart has finished love for me. She shed a few tears for her lost love and her anger at Adrian's behaviour, and, not least, for her willingness to respond to his kiss.

*   *   *

When her doorbell rang the next evening, Jennie's first thought was that it must be Adrian back again, perhaps wanting to apologise. She hurried downstairs and opened the door to a tall, young woman of about thirty. Jennie frowned for a moment, thinking that the visitor was not unlike Amanda.

'I'm sorry,' she began to say, but the

stranger interrupted quickly.

'You don't know me. I am a friend of Adrian Challis and I would like to speak to you. Do you mind if I come in?'

'Oh, I suppose so. Come upstairs.'

Jennie was puzzled, but went quickly upstairs and showed the girl into the living-room.

'I don't understand,' she said.

'No, I don't suppose you do, but I believe in speaking frankly and I'll say what I've got to say and then we'll know where we stand.'

They both sat down and Jennie found that she rather liked the look of the girl. Although her voice had an edge to it, the lines of her face were friendly, and she was rather nice-looking in a striking kind of way.

'I am Lorna Stewart and I run Adrian's shop in Perth. He may have mentioned me.'

'You mean you are the Lorna who—' Jennie began, but was interrupted.

'Yes, I know what you are thinking. Adrian and I have lived together for some years and I know Adrian very well. I also know that every so often, he gets attracted by a young girl such as yourself.'

'And Fiona,' Jennie put in.

'Yes, well, I was sorry about Fiona, but it all turned out for the best and she is happy at university now.' She looked at Jennie with a hard, purposeful stare. 'I will come to the point. When Adrian starts staying away for two evenings every week, I know I don't have far to look, and he had told me of the young person who had taken charge of the Kingowan shop.

'Last night, he was very late home and not in a good temper either, so I thought it was time to come over and see you. I happen to love Adrian, you see, and I'm not giving him up easily. I wanted you to understand that.'

Jennie started to laugh. In the first place, she rather liked this Lorna and the way she was sticking up for Adrian; and then she was remembering the scene of the night before and how it had ended.

'Lorna,' she said, 'you've been honest with me and I will be the same with you. I was getting to like Adrian. He was good company and I'd just been through a bad patch. I've been cooking him a meal on his day over here and we've been out to dinner once or twice. Then he started coming over on another evening and we would go for a walk. Well, last night, we got caught in the rain, and he came back here to dry off. To my horror, he began to show a little too much attention, and of course he tried it on.'

'But . . .'

'No, let me tell you. He wanted to stay the night and he kissed me, but I told him to go. I don't think he was very pleased. I'm sorry if he's unfaithful to you, but you seem to know him better than I do.'

Lorna was smiling now. 'You mean you gave

him the brush-off?' She chuckled. 'It must be the first time anyone's turned him down. I think I'm going to like you, Jennie.'

'Will you have some coffee, or a drink?'

'Coffee would be fine. I mustn't stay too long. It's Adrian's day for Braemar and he's always back late.'

Jennie looked at her with mischief in her eyes. 'And who is in charge of the shop at Braemar?'

Lorna grinned. 'Oh, I think I'm safe there. It's a respectable, married lady like Mrs Cameron who was here. Adrian only seems to go for the young faces.'

'You're very loyal to him.'

'I'm a fool, but love sometimes makes fools of us.' Lorna followed Jennie into the kitchen. 'Are you married, Jennie? You obviously didn't welcome Adrian's advances.'

Jennie spoke over her shoulder as she made the coffee.

'Yes, I was married, but my husband was seeing someone else and I didn't even suspect. I was a fool, too. I'm divorcing him.'

'I'm sorry, but you'll meet someone else. You're still young enough. You obviously didn't love him very much as you don't sound very heartbroken.'

They carried their coffee through.

'That's the odd thing,' Jennie said. 'I find it hard to understand. I was really in love with him to begin with, but don't even seem to miss him, though I'm not in the least keen to meet someone else.'

'Oh, well, you've taken a load off my mind,' Lorna said. 'I'll have peace of mind when I know it's Adrian's Kingowan day in future. I don't expect he'll stop trying though, Jennie. He doesn't like to be thwarted.'

'Don't you mind not being married to him?' Jennie queried.

'No. He says he's not the marrying type. Doesn't want to be tied down I suppose, though he's stayed with me for eight years.' Lorna seemed to accept her situation quite philosophically and cheerfully. 'Do you like the shop, Jennie? You seem to have settled in very quickly.'

'Yes, I love it and I was lucky getting a shop with a flat above it. It's nice, isn't it?'

Lorna looked around her. 'Funnily enough, I've never been up here before. Mrs Cameron didn't use it and before that there was an old spinster running the shop whom I didn't get on with very well. She was here when Adrian bought it so he was stuck with her. But I must be going. Perhaps you'd like to come over and see the Perth shop one day. It's three times the size of Kingowan and I've got an assistant.'

'No problems with her?'

Lorna laughed as she got up and walked towards the door.

'No, she got married a few months back. Thanks for the coffee, Jennie, and I'm glad we didn't have to fall out about Adrian.'

'Oh, Lorna, I wish you the best of luck.'

After Lorna had gone, Jennie sat down. She was in a relaxed frame of mind and she found she was thinking of Ian. She had seen very little of him, no more than a wave and to pass the time of day when they were opening or closing the shops, but he had been right to warn her about Adrian.

It worried Jennie slightly that he might still try to pursue his romantic inclinations on his next visit, but when the day came, the van pulled up and he was all smiles.

'Hello, Jennie! Have you forgiven me for my attack on your virtue? And I hear you had a visitor the next night! You needn't look confused. Lorna told me all about it. I thought the two of you might get on rather well together.'

'I thought Lorna was a very nice person, Adrian.'

'She is, one of the best and she has a lot to put up with.' He was quite unashamed and put his arm round Jennie's waist as they went into the shop.

'If I promise to behave myself, my sweet Jennie, will you still come out to dinner with me occasionally? I enjoyed those evenings.'

'I will if you promise to tell Lorna where you are,' she replied.

'Yes, I daresay I could do that and I know that Lorna won't mind now that she has met you.' He stopped in the doorway. 'But now, down to business. I've brought you some pictures and some small pieces of silver, salt-cellars and cream jugs. But the prize piece is carefully wrapped up in the van. You'll have to help me with it.'

They carried the small items in and then Adrian pointed to a large object covered in cloths.

'Lift it carefully. You will see what it is when we get into the shop.'

It was very heavy, Jennie found out as they manoeuvred it through the doorway with great care and carried it down to the back of the shop.

'I don't want it in the window,' Adrian said. 'It's rather special.'

He took off the cloths to reveal the gleaming mahogany of a handsome chest of drawers. Jennie drew in her breath.

'Adrian! It's beautiful. It must be worth thousands.'

He nodded. 'Yes, you're right. Now try and guess the date.'

She was thoughtful as she opened the drawers, looking at the joints. She saw that it had the original drop handles.

'Is it George the Third?' she ventured.

'Right first time, young lady, full marks. Isn't it perfect?'

'But it's in such wonderful condition,' she remarked.

He laughed. 'It wasn't, but I've had it polished so there's no patina, which is a pity But look at the handles, just as they were. You can guess who's going to be interested, can't you?'

'Colonel Fairfax.'

'Yes, Colonel Fairfax. It's worth six thousand pounds, but if he's willing to write a cheque, he can have it for five-and-a-half. Will you ring him tomorrow and tell him? I don't want to stop too long today as I've got to get over to Pitlochry. You'll take care of it, won't you? And if he does buy it, make sure it's well wrapped up in the cloths.'

He left soon after that and Jennie felt excited for the rest of the day. She gave the chest a rub down with a duster and in the afternoon, she phoned Colonel Fairfax. She was told he was away for a day or two and would be back on Friday and she felt quite disappointed.

Her thoughts were far from her personal life and her problems as she prepared to lock up that night, and she was rather alarmed when, just before closing time, the shop bell rang and a man stepped into the shop.

She hurried forward and then stopped in astonishment.

'Hello, Jennie.'

It was Stuart!

CHAPTER FOUR

Stuart held out a hand to Jennie, but she ignored it. She kept looking at the face that had once been so familiar, but he seemed a stranger. She didn't know what to say to him.

'Well, aren't you pleased to see me, Jennie?'

She busied herself locking the door and setting the alarm, trying to hide the feeling of dismay she felt that he should have sought her out.

'How did you know where to find me?' she asked rather abruptly.

'I went round to see your mother. She wasn't there, but Katrina told me you were working here. Your address was on the divorce petition, but I didn't realise you were working and living in the same place.'

He sounded confident, with an air of intimacy about him, as though nothing had happened to disturb their relationship.

'Why have you come?' Jennie enquired.

'You don't sound very pleased to see me and it's ages since I saw you. I want to talk to you, Jennie.'

She started to walk through the shop.

'Well, you'd better come up to the flat. We can't talk here.'

Stuart was looking around him. 'You've got some nice stuff here, Jennie. You always did like antiques, didn't you?'

She didn't reply as he followed her upstairs. With every step she took, she felt uneasy. She went straight into the kitchen.

'Go into the living-room, Stuart. I'll bring some coffee.'

When she joined him and put the cups down on the small table, she noticed that he was standing at the bookcase.

'You've still got all your books, I see,' he remarked.

'Of course I have.'

'My shelves seemed rather empty after you had gone. Amanda doesn't like reading.'

Jennie looked at him with some disbelief. He had the nerve to mention Amanda! Whatever was it all about, she wondered. The only thing to do was to ask him outright.

'Stuart, I can't pretend I'm pleased to see you, because I'm not. I'm just managing to put the past behind me and make a new life for myself . . .'

He interrupted quickly. 'Have you found a new boyfriend then, Jenny?'

'No, I haven't and it's nothing to do with you in any case. Are you going to tell me why you have come here. You can't pretend you were just passing through because you didn't even know where I worked.'

He put down his coffee cup and leaned towards her, his expression anxious.

'Jennie, I've come to ask you if you will have

me back. Could we cancel the divorce proceedings and try and make a new start together?' The words sounded loud in the quiet room. Jennie went rigid with shock and amazement.

'You can't be serious.'

'I am very serious. I know now I made a mistake. I treated you badly, but I still love you, Jennie, and I was hoping you'd say you still loved me.'

She stared at him. The feeling that she was facing a stranger wouldn't leave her. The man sitting in front of her, saying these incredible words, couldn't be the Stuart she had loved and married. She felt angry.

'But what on earth has happened? You have Amanda and that's what you wanted, isn't it? How on earth can you talk of us getting back together again? It was Amanda you loved.'

He tried to take her hand but she pulled hers away.

'Please, listen to me, Jennie. I know I behaved badly, but I was hoping to make you understand. I was dazzled by Amanda. I think she bewitched me. I could think of nothing else but being with her. I was so sure she was the love of my life and that I had been wrong to marry someone as young as you—'

'But what's happened?' She was almost screaming at him. 'Are you going to tell me what has happened now?'

'What has happened is that it didn't work

out with Amanda. Working with her all day and living with her as well just wasn't a good idea. We found out very quickly we couldn't live together and she moved back to her own house before it was sold. I've missed you, Jennie. I thought I'd made one big mess of things, then I began to wonder if you were missing me, too. I thought perhaps you still loved me and would come back to me. What do you think, Jennie? Would you give it a try?'

Jennie took a deep breath to try and control her temper. Although she felt confused by what was happening, one thing stood out very clearly in her mind. The last thing she wanted in her life was to go back and live with Stuart. She could never trust him again and without trust, how could there be any love?

She looked at him. He was the same Stuart, but he wasn't the Stuart she had loved when she was in her teens. Somehow, in that year of estrangement when he had been involved with Amanda, he had succeeded in killing any love she had felt for him. She even wondered if she had truly loved him in the first place or whether it had been the infatuation of a young girl for an older, attractive man.

While all these thoughts raced through her mind, she hadn't noticed that Stuart had crossed to her and was now reaching out to take hold of her hands. Suddenly, she was in his arms and he was kissing her. For a quick second, she remembered an old magic, but it

51

was no more than a betrayal of her senses and as she pushed him away, her head cleared and her mind knew with a sharp, clear decision that she did not want Stuart's kisses, did not want Stuart's love.

'No, Stuart, no.' Any hesitation was gone. 'I'm not coming back to you. It's all over and I don't love you any more. You spoiled it all and you will have to take the consequences.'

'But, Jennie, I promise you I wouldn't be unfaithful to you again. It would be like that first year when we were so happy. I want it to be like that all over again.'

'I dare say you do,' she said sarcastically. 'You should have thought of that when you first started seeing Amanda. You can't turn back the clock, Stuart. I was only twenty then and I trusted you. I was a fool and I know it now and I'm not going to make the same mistake again.'

'But, Jennie, you might at least give it a try. I do love you and if I hurt you, I am sorry, but I am sure we could pick up where we left off.'

'Well, you are wrong, Stuart Graham, and you are so conceited. I don't love you any more and I don't even think I like you.'

'Jennie, think it over, please. I'll come back next week and we'll talk again.'

'I don't want you to come back and I don't want to talk to you again. My mind is quite made up and nothing you can say will change it. Now, I think you'd better go.' Jennie started walking towards the door.

'You'll regret it, Jennie, my dear. You'll be all on your own when you could have been comfortable back with me. I've got a good mind to contest the divorce. There's still time.' He was shouting at her now.

Jennie laughed out loud. 'You can contest it as much as you like. I have named Amanda and you can't deny what happened. I'll be glad to see the last of you and you'd better not come here again.'

He stalked off down the stairs without another word, and he was through the shop, struggling with the front door before she could stop him, but not before the burglar alarm rang out. She ran through the shop and turned it off just as Stuart was getting into his car and roaring up the road.

With tears in her eyes, she locked up again and hurried back upstairs. At that moment, her doorbell rang. Whatever is it going to be next, she wondered as she returned downstairs.

She brushed the tears from her eyes before reaching the back door. When she opened it, she was surprised to find there none other than Ian McWilliam.

'Jennie,' His voice, firm and deep with more than a hint of concern, broke her control.

'Oh, Ian!'

Without saying a word, he came in and shut the door behind him as Jennie flung herself into his arms and burst into loud sobs. He held her gently, full of care, stroking her hair and murmuring her name over and over again. She felt a great sense of comfort and, gradually, she managed to pull herself together and stop crying.

'I'm sorry, Ian! I don't know what you must think of me,' she said quietly, still held in his arms. 'Why did you come, just at that very minute? I was really in need of a manly chest to cry on!'

Ian was very serious. 'I was worried, Jennie. Just as we were locking up, I saw a man come into the shop. When he disappeared and didn't come out again, it made me feel uneasy. Then, as time went past and his car was still there, I thought it must be someone you know. But when I heard the burglar alarm give a short ring, I just had to see what was wrong. I'm sorry if I'm intruding into something private and I'll go if you'd prefer it. Are you all right now, Jennie?'

She nodded and gave him a watery smile.

'I have never been so glad to see anyone in all my life, Ian. I was just going to get myself a drink. Would you have one with me?'

'Yes, if you like, and if you want to unburden yourself, I'd like you to think that you could speak to me in confidence.'

'Thanks, Ian. Come on up.'

Once in the living-room, Jennie went over to her sideboard.

'I've only got Martini and tonic. Will that do, Ian?'

'Fine,' he said. 'Do you want me to pour?'

'Thanks. I'll wash my face and comb my hair, if you don't object.'

'You look lovely as you are, Jennie.'

'Ian!'

He laughed. 'I was being quite sincere and not trying to flatter. I always did think your hair was beautiful when I was younger. You were just a young girl then and wore it quite long.'

'I think you are going to be good for me, Ian. I won't tell you what I used to think about you! I didn't like you at all.' She laughed, feeling quite relaxed again.

'Oh, dear, what had I done to deserve that?' he asked.

She looked at him and suddenly saw his fine, sensitive features quite differently. He was really very attractive.

'I always thought you were very superior and stand-offish, and you never seemed to smile. I was afraid to come into the shop!'

'I'm sorry. I think I did take myself very seriously in those days. I was terrified I'd done the wrong thing putting all my small savings into a second-hand bookshop.'

'But you've been successful, haven't you?'

'I can't grumble.' He smiled. 'I have quite a good catalogue and do a lot by post. However, that's by the way. I hope you've got over your prejudice and that you are going to tell me what's troubling you. Is there anything I can do to help?'

She shook her head. 'No, thank you, it's my past rearing its ugly head.'

'Jennie, you can't have a past. You're barely into your twenties, surely.'

'Old enough to have a failed marriage and a divorce on the way. I think I mentioned it before.'

'Yes, and I'm sorry. The man who drove away so angrily just now—who was that?'

'That was Stuart, my husband. I still can't believe it, but he came to ask me to go back with him.'

'And you didn't want to?' Ian inquired gently.

'No, I don't want to at all. He went off with another woman, Ian, and it hasn't worked out for them. So he thinks he can put it all back together again with me. But, you see . . .'

She looked at the intent face in front of her. I can trust him, she thought.

'I know this might sound silly,' she continued, 'but I suddenly looked at him tonight and I didn't love him any more. It was gone, finished, almost as though I'd never known or loved him at all. He was like a stranger to me.'

Ian was thoughtful for a moment. 'And is the divorce to go ahead?'

'Yes, but now there are complications.

Stuart says he will contest it and I would have to go to court. I thought I was going to avoid all that, having everything done through solicitors.' Jennie sounded troubled.

'Don't worry too much. If you are sure it's what you want and you say you don't love Stuart any more, you won't find it too much of an ordeal.' Ian got up and prepared to go. 'Will you be all right now?'

'Yes, thank you. I think you saved my life.'

'Jennie, do you like walking?'

'Walking?' she repeated rather stupidly.

'Yes, up on the hills, walking-boots and cagoul stuff, I mean.'

Jennie smiled. 'I used to love it when I was a youngster, but I haven't walked any distance for years. Why do you ask?'

'I often go out on a Sunday and I wondered if you would like to come with me—when your divorce is through, that is. I don't want to cause any complications. Can I ask you again?'

'I'd love to, Ian. Thanks very much for asking.'

'That's fine. Just let me know as soon as you are free and we'll fix up something. I'll look forward to it.' He stopped at the top of the stairs. 'And, Jennie, you'll come over if you have any trouble, won't you?'

'Yes, I will, though I don't think Stuart will come back again. It's only a matter of weeks before the divorce will be heard. 'Bye, Ian, and thank you again.'

His smile lit up his eyes. 'Goodbye, Jennie, take care.'

Upstairs again, Jennie suddenly felt hungry so decided to get herself something to eat. Ian kept creeping into her thoughts and she realised that she was almost seeing him now for the first time.

In the disturbance, she had forgotten to phone Colonel Fairfax about the chest of drawers, but when she finally spoke to him, he sounded quite excited and said that he would come into Kingowan that afternoon. When he did arrive, he was driving a large estate van, which made Jennie think he had hopes of taking the chest back with him.

She greeted him eagerly and led him through to the back of the shop. She saw his eyes light up but he didn't say anything and she stood and silently watched while he examined the chest carefully.

'It's beautiful,' he said slowly when he'd satisfied himself. 'Almost too beautiful and little sign of wear.'

'Adrian said it was in very poor shape and he got someone to polish it,' Jennie told the colonel who was running his fingers along the top of the chest lovingly.

'Did he mention a date? It's definitely George the Third but he can possibly get nearer than I can.'

'He said about 1775, I think.'

'Yes, quite early, I thought. I don't know

why I'm hesitating. Adrian knew I would like it and he was quite right. It's not a reproduction, is it?'

'Reproduction?' Jennie was horrified. 'Adrian doesn't deal in reproduction furniture, Colonel Fairfax. You know that.'

'Yes, I do know that. I'm sorry, I don't know what made me say it. What is he asking for it?'

Jennie told him the price and the terms.

'That's fair, fair,' he said. 'I can't resist it, can I?' He took a cheque book from his pocket. 'That won't bounce,' he said jokingly as he handed her the completed cheque. 'Can you give me some cloths or something, Jennie?'

'Are you going to take it now?'

'Yes, I brought the van just in case.'

'I've got the cloths Adrian brought the chest in. We'll have to be careful.'

Between them, they succeeded in getting the precious piece of furniture into the estate van. When Jennie had waved goodbye to the colonel, she went back into the shop feeling well satisfied. She put the cheque into the safe and decided to telephone Adrian that evening to let him know the good news.

When she did speak to him, Jennie thought he sounded slightly wary. She had expected him to be overjoyed.

'Have you got the cheque safe, Jennie? You haven't put it into the bank?'

'There wasn't time to take it to the bank

after Colonel Fairfax had gone. I've put it in the safe.'

'Well, leave it there until I come. I might pop over on Sunday to collect it. Will you be in?'

'Morning or afternoon, Adrian?'

'Early afternoon, I should think, about two o'clock. I'll look forward to seeing you. Goodbye, Jennie.'

She was puzzled as she put the phone down. He was worried about something, almost jumpy, she thought. I wonder if it's something to do with the cheque? Surely he knows the colonel well enough by now to trust him. Oh, well, I shall see on Sunday. Perhaps he'll be happier to have the cheque in his own hands.

When Sunday came, Jennie found that she was quite pleased that she was going to see Adrian. Then she started to question her thoughts—he behaves outrageously and I put him in his place then I find myself looking forward to seeing him! I must be mad! Either that or Adrian Challis really does know how to charm. But I must remember Lorna, she reminded herself. She's stuck by him all this time and I'm not going to cause any damage to that relationship.

Sunday had turned into a very hot day and Jennie found herself wishing that Adrian would take her to the river or at least somewhere cool and shady. She dressed in her thinnest, sleeveless dress and tried to find the coolest place in the flat. It was actually cooler down in the shop than anywhere else and she thought she might as well be doing a little tidying while she was waiting for Adrian to arrive.

As she went through into the shop, she caught sight of Ian across the road. He was in the window of the bookshop, obviously making a new display. She walked across the road and he saw her, disappeared and then came out of the shop door.

'Busy on a Sunday, Ian?' she greeted him.

'It's the only chance I get to do the window and it was too hot to go walking today. What are you doing with yourself?'

'Adrian's coming over. There was something urgent for him to pick up.'

A frown clouded Ian's clear eyes. 'Coming to see you on a Sunday, is he? Don't forget my warning, Jennie.'

She had to laugh. 'I can cope with the Adrians of this world, Ian. I had another warning, too. Lorna came to see me.'

'Did she now? So you know I wasn't making it all up?'

'It's not like you to invent stories like that,' she replied. 'I am sure of that.' She looked up at his troubled face and smiled at him. 'Stop worrying. I've got Adrian's measure and won't come to any harm.'

He grinned. 'I feel as though I'm your protector, but I don't think you want to be protected. Have a nice afternoon, Jennie. I can see Adrian coming now.'

Jennie hurried back to the shop and waited for Adrian's car to pull up. She could tell at once that he was in a good humour, but, nevertheless, his first words, after giving her a brief kiss on the cheek, were concerning the chest of drawers.

'Did the colonel take the chest safely, Jennie? You haven't heard that it came to any harm.'

'No, everything is fine. I'll get the cheque for you.'

'No, leave it in the safe until I go. Shall we go out, Jennie, find somewhere cool under the trees? Would you like that?'

'Oh, yes, I would, Adrian.' Pleasure sounded in Jennie's voice. 'I was hoping you would suggest it.'

'Let's lock up then and we'll go up to Rachan Forest. I know a nice, quiet place up there on the hillside where there is sure to be a lovely, cool breeze.'

Once they were out of the town and on the road towards the loch, Adrian suddenly turned off on to a steep, forest track that Jennie had never seen before. It seemed dark and gloomy in the densely-packed trees after being in the bright sunshine, but after five minutes driving, he pulled up in a clearing and Jennie could see that from there, they would have views over Loch Torvie and the surrounding hills.

Now in good spirits, Adrian took a rug from the car and they walked to the edge of the trees. He spread it down in a shady place and Jennie sat down with a great deal of delight when she saw the views and felt the stir of the breeze on her face.

'Oh, it's lovely, Adrian. I've never been up here before, yet I've lived here all my life.'

He smiled at her, taking pleasure in the clear, innocent joy that showed in her face.

'It's worth exploring these tracks. No-one else ever seems to find them. They all go to the loch like bees to a honey-pot.'

She nodded. 'We used to cycle to the loch when we were children. It was always a popular place.'

'You don't regret moving from Edinburgh then, Jennie? You are quite happy in Kingowan and with the shop?'

'Yes, thanks. I love it. I'm glad I came home,' she said.

'So am I.'

She looked at him quickly but his face showed nothing but friendliness and a kind concern. It did not prepare her for his next move.

'I am very glad, Jennie, and I wanted to tell you today that I am coming to love you very much.' As he spoke, his arm encircled her waist, forcing her back to lie on the rug. His lips sought the softness at her neck, his hands holding her arms to stop her rising.

Jennie tried to sit up but it seemed to inflame Adrian and his hand slipped behind her head to bring her face closer to his. It was a passionate kiss and it aroused feelings in her body that Jennie did not want to admit to for this man.

'No, Adrian,' she exclaimed suddenly.

'Jennie, I love you and I want you so much.'

Jennie knew she must keep talking if she was to be free of him.

'I don't love you in that way, Adrian, and I've no intention of being one of the young girls you take up with from time to time.'

'Jennie, it's not like that this time, believe me. I love you very much and I would like to marry you when you are free.'

CHAPTER FIVE

Jennie sat up quickly at his words. She found herself staring at Adrian unable to believe the words she had just heard. Her first thoughts were of Lorna.

'Marriage, Adrian, from you? And what about Lorna?' she asked scornfully.

He took her hands in his, looking very serious.

'Jennie, listen to me, just a minute. Don't try to stop me. Lorna and I have been good friends for many years, but she knows that I don't love her in that way. She has accepted our relationship and I suppose we have been happy in our own way. But I always knew, I always hoped, that perhaps one day, I would meet the girl I wanted to marry.

'And I have, Jennie. I love you with the kind of feeling I have never had for any other girl. There's nothing I want more than for you to be my wife. I know you don't dislike me, but you are still entangled. Please say that you will think of marrying me when you are free.'

Jennie had listened to him without interruption, her hands still clasped in his. His words had seemed out of character and she wondered if this was an Adrian she had yet to discover. For moments, she felt sorry for him which seemed strange as she also felt sorry for

Lorna. She would have to choose her words carefully.

'I suppose, in an old-fashioned kind of way, I should be thanking you for asking me to marry you. But the answer is no, Adrian. It always will be no. I don't feel that I ever want to marry again. Trusting a man is very hard when you've been let down once.'

'But, Jennie, I would—'

'No, let me have my say. I keep thinking of Lorna. She loves you very much, is nearer to you in age and you have the interest of the business in common. It's Lorna you should be asking to marry you.'

'No, Jennie.' He was shaking his head. 'I don't love Lorna in that way. I am fond of her but as soon as you came along, I knew it was no more than fondness and that it was you I loved. I think I knew straight away when you came for your interview. But, Jennie, I can wait. You don't have to make up your mind now. Wait until the divorce is over and you feel free. You may think differently then.'

'I would never marry without love, Adrian. I was in love with Stuart, but it all fell apart, so what chance has a marriage without love got? Try and forget about me.'

'I can't forget you, Jennie, and I am sure I could make you love me.'

But she continued to protest. 'Love isn't like that, Adrian, and I don't wish to hear you talking like this again. It could mean that I'm

66

going to have to leave the shop. How can we go on if you are forever pestering me to love you?'

'It won't be like that, I promise you. I shall look forward to seeing you once a week, and, in a year's time, I'll bring you back to this very spot and ask you again!'

Jennie was grateful for the reprieve for she had no idea how she could convince him that she did not want to marry him; neither did she want to give up her job and her flat.

'Thank you, Adrian,' she said. 'Perhaps you will see things as I do in a year's time.'

'And perhaps you will agree with me!' He smiled and pulled her to her feet. 'Just one kiss to show that we are still friends, Jennie.'

She laughed and lifted her face to his. The kiss was brief and gentle. They said very little as they drove back to Kingowan, and in the flat, Jennie made some tea before Adrian set off to return to Perth.

After he had gone, she felt tired and almost puzzled by the events of the afternoon. It had all been so unexpected and she wondered if it was the true Adrian she was seeing. Gone was the smiling charm of the successful business man. He had seemed genuinely sincere when he had told her he loved her.

Somewhere deep within her, though, there nagged the cynical thought that Adrian was capable of putting on his feelings to suit the occasion. How was he going to behave towards

Lorna when he returned to Perth? How would he behave the next time he came over to Kingowan?

Jennie was to ask herself these questions many times during the next few weeks for she found Adrian to be in an odd mood when he came over to the shop. He would give her a hug when he arrived and seemed pleased to see her, and when he left, he gave her a quick, light kiss, said, 'Still love you, Jennie' and was gone. But in between, he seemed on edge and uneasy, slightly distracted, as though he had something else on his mind.

Adrian and his strange behaviour was driven from her mind, however, by the arrival of a letter from the court giving her the date of the divorce proceedings and asking her to attend. Adrian was sympathetic and told her that she could shut up the shop for as long as was necessary.

When the week of the hearing came, she went across to tell Ian. She hadn't seen a lot of him, but she knew that he would worry if he saw that the shop was closed unexpectedly.

'I'm glad you haven't to wait any longer,' he said when she told him. 'I haven't said a lot about it, but I know you'll be glad to have it behind you. I hope all goes well for you.'

*   *   *

The morning that Jennie drove to court, she

was a bag of nerves and was thankful that her mother was sitting calmly by her side. She kept thinking of Stuart and, in particular, of their last quarrel.

He had never returned, she said to herself. I must have convinced him, or, I wonder if he thinks because he is contesting the divorce that I won't get it and then he'll still be married to me. Her solicitor had tried to reassure her, but the worries wouldn't go away and she started to talk to her mother about the shop, about Katrina, about anything that didn't remind her of the ordeal ahead.

The scenes in the court were to remain hazy for ever for Jennie. She remembered an angry, stony-faced Stuart, a glimpse of Amanda and a kindly judge. She was granted her decree nisi without any bother and she stood outside the court building, dazed, clinging to her mother's hand, unable to believe that it was all over. It had all been like an unpleasant dream.

Mrs McLeod looked at her daughter, still so young.

'What will you do now, Jennie?' she asked as soon as they were free of the town's traffic.

'Stay at the shop, of course, as long as Adrian isn't going to be a nuisance. I like it there and I can afford to live quite comfortably and keep on the car. I'm very lucky really.'

'You don't seem to have any regrets about Stuart.'

'No. You were right to start off with, Mum.

You said I was too young to get married, but I wouldn't listen to you, would I? However, that chapter in my life is definitely closed from now on.'

Back in Kingowan, as soon as Jennie had opened the shop, Ian came hurrying over, looking quite anxious.

'How did it go, Jennie? Is everything all right?'

'Fine thank you, Ian. I'll be a free woman in six weeks' time.'

'Good girl. I just wanted to make sure you were all right.' He looked at her as though trying to guess her mood. 'Jennie, I didn't know how you would be feeling and I thought perhaps you wouldn't want to be on your own this evening, so I've bought a few things for a meal. Would you come over and have supper with me?'

Jennie met his grey eyes. 'Oh, Ian, you are kind. I'd love to come. What time shall we say?'

'About seven. Will that do?'

'Yes, fine,' she said. 'And, Ian, thank you.'

She was in an unusual state of excitement as she got ready to go over to Ian. It's like starting a new life, she said to herself. Stuart was part of the past and here she was getting ready to spend an evening with Ian, who, although he might not be part of the future, was turning out to be a very good friend.

The houses on the opposite side of Crieff

70

Road were quite different from the old cottages that had been turned into small shops. The bookshop was one in a row of tall, Regency, terraced houses, some of them turned into shops, some of them offices but none of them private houses. Jennie knew that Ian lived above the shop but had no idea what kind of accommodation he had.

He opened the shop door to let her in and, although he smiled, Jennie felt that there was an air of reserve about him. Perhaps he isn't used to entertaining young ladies, she chuckled to herself. At the side of the shop, a staircase led up to the first floor and she gave a gasp when she reached the top and saw that it opened into a room running the whole length of the house, with windows at each end.

Jennie enjoyed everything about that evening—the carefully-prepared salad, followed by fresh fruit and cheese, the good wine Ian served with it and then his insistence that the washing-up could wait until the morning. Then he gave her the chance to talk about what had happened at the court, proving to be a good listener.

'Are you going to be able to put it behind you now, Jennie?' he asked her when she had finished.

'I think so,' she replied. 'It just seems an enormous relief. It certainly makes me feel that I never want to get married again.'

'What about Adrian?'

'Adrian?' In her surprise at his question, she could only echo the name.

'Yes, he's very keen on you, isn't he?'

She pulled a face. 'I don't know how you know. I suspect you've been spying'

'No, I wouldn't do that, Jennie, but sometimes I have been opening up when he has arrived and his greeting seems more than affectionate. I wondered if he was up to his old tricks again. I wouldn't like to see you hurt.'

Jennie shook her head. 'You don't have to worry about me, Ian. I'm more than able to cope with Adrian, though you're not entirely right about him. He actually asked me to marry him.'

Ian's expression was comical. 'I don't believe it!' He paused. 'And what did you say?'

'I turned him down. He says he'll ask me again in a year's time. He seemed really serious, not a bit like him. But I shouldn't be talking about Adrian like this. It is very wrong of me. Let's change the subject!'

'Would you like to come walking with me one day, Jennie? I did ask you before and you seemed quite keen,' Ian asked. 'We'll wait until the cooler days of September. Would that be all right with you?'

'Yes, thank you, that's lovely. We can celebrate my divorce becoming absolute! I shall be free and would love to come with you, Ian, though I'm not sure that I'll be up to your pace.'

72

'We'll do an easy walk to start off with, to break you in.'

His words made her smile, for he had spoken as though the walk was to be one of many. Jennie rather liked the feeling and went home thinking what a nice end to a difficult day it had been.

*   *   *

Jennie was to see very little of Ian or Adrian during the next few weeks. It was the height of the holiday season and she was very busy in the shop.

Adrian kept the stock well topped up each week but he brought no more larger items of valuable furniture. He still seemed edgy and off-hand, but she knew it was a very busy time for him, too, and that he was spending every day going to the different shops and attending the vital sales in between.

They had one evening out together, a dinner at their favourite hotel and a walk along the shores of the loch afterwards.

'Do you know, I haven't seen Colonel Fairfax once since he bought that chest,' Jennie said. 'At one time, he didn't miss a week.'

She found her arm clutched and he brought her round to face him. She saw the anxiety in his eyes and couldn't understand it.

'You haven't seen him at all?' His voice was

sharp and strident.

'No. I'd got used to having a chat with him every week and showing him what you'd brought in, even if he didn't buy anything.'

There was a long silence and Jennie could tell from the look on Adrian's face that something was wrong. Surely the business in his shops couldn't be so bad that Adrian would miss a regular customer like the colonel?

She didn't know why, but she felt almost protective towards him.

'Don't worry if the colonel hasn't been in, Adrian. Perhaps he avoids the town at the height of the tourist season. A lot of local people do, or perhaps he's away on holiday. Bring in something else to tempt him and he'll soon be back.'

The hug he gave her almost stopped her breath and she started to laugh.

'You are a darling, Jennie Graham, my very own darling, and I love you still!'

'Adrian, you promised.'

'I know, but it suddenly came over me again when you showed such understanding.'

Encouraging him was the last thing Jennie had intended and she regretted her impulsive, sympathetic action. But Adrian had recovered his spirits, and, during the drive back to Kingowan, he was deliberately and audaciously loving until she had to laugh at him and told him not to worry about the shop. She would do her best.

On the sixth of September, Jennie received the notice that her divorce was now absolute. She raced over to tell Ian, who couldn't hide his delight. They planned a walk for the following Sunday.

When Sunday arrived, Jennie joined Ian at the front of the shop. The weather had turned cooler and the air was inclined to dampness, but no rain was forecast so they hoped for a good day.

Jennie was surprised when they drove out of Kingowan and Ian went straight down the Crieff Road and headed into the southern hills. When the road eventually ran out into a green track, Ian stopped the car and turned to her, grinning.

'This is as far as I can bring you, Jennie, but the way I've planned is not too steep.' He pointed to the hill in front of them. 'We take a path along the side of the hill, through that gap, then upwards. You'll love it up there and then, of course, it's downhill all the way back! Are you game?'

'I am indeed,' she said stoutly and hitched her rucksack over her shoulders.

Ian walked ahead and Jennie soon realised he had set a sensible pace that she could manage. They climbed steadily and she found that she got only slightly short of breath. Once, Ian stopped and let her catch him up and they sat down to admire the view, with Ian pointing out the various landmarks.

When he stood up, he held out a hand to her, pulling her to her feet with a laugh. Jennie was very conscious of the firm grip of his hand. They walked steadily and silently for nearly an hour, then the path turned steeply upwards and, once again, Jennie found herself catching her breath. She joined Ian at the top, panting and groaning but trying to laugh it off.

'You're a brute!' she teased him. 'I don't think I shall come walking with you again!'

'Oh, Jennie, don't say that.' There was dismay in his tone and it made her laugh again. 'Just look at the view. Wasn't it worth it?'

Jennie looked at Ian with shining eyes. 'Oh, it's so beautiful. Thanks for bringing me.'

'And will you come with me again?' She knew he was teasing her.

'I won't be able to say no, will I? Not after this, and as you said, it's downhill all the way back.'

They ate their sandwiches with their backs propped up against the huge boulders at the top, protected from the wind. Jennie was very conscious of a joyful sense of being alive and able to share the same feelings with the man at her side; they said little, but she felt complete harmony between them. This is one of the happiest moments of my life, she said to herself. I never remember feeling quite like this before. I shall never forget it.

At last, Ian broke the spell and said the words she didn't really want to hear.

'We must be making our way back now, Jennie. Are you fit?'

She smiled at him. 'Yes, but I don't want to leave. I could stay here for ever.'

'In two hours' time, you would start to feel very cold,' Ian replied.

Jennie managed to keep up a good pace all the way back though the last mile found her legs feeling rather like jelly and she knew that she would be very stiff the next day. She didn't speak until they were back in Kingowan.

'Thanks for a lovely day. I hope I didn't slow you up too much.'

He glanced at her. 'It's given me a lot of pleasure to have you with me, Jennie, and I hope we can do it again soon.'

Next day, she was tidying the shop at the end of a busy day when the door opened and she assumed it to be a late customer. A tall man with grey hair walked across the shop towards her. As he reached her, he held out a card.

'Detective Inspector Baillie, CID. I am looking for Mr Adrian Challis. Is he here?'

CHAPTER SIX

Jennie knew immediately that there was something wrong. They sometimes had visits from the CID looking for stolen goods, but the attitude of this inspector was quite different from those of his colleagues who, in the past, had been seeking co-operation from her or from Adrian.

'Mr Challis is not here,' she replied nervously. 'He comes on a Wednesday, as a rule. Is something wrong?'

'I am not in a position to say at the moment,' was the stiff reply. 'I need to see Mr Challis urgently. Can you tell me where I can contact him?'

Jennie frowned. 'I've no idea where he will be at this moment. There are other shops, you see, or he could be at a sale or an auction.'

'Is this his main shop? Does he live here?'

She shook her head. 'No, I live in the flat above the shop. The main shop is in Perth and Mr Challis has a house there.' Even as she spoke, Jennie wondered if she was saying too much. Was Adrian in trouble? Whatever could have happened?

She was hardly given time to think by the inspector who was already on his way down the shop towards the office.

'Is there a phone here, and could I have the

number of the Perth shop, please? Who will I be speaking to?'

'Lorna Stewart is in charge there.'

Jennie listened to the brief conversation and sensed from the inspector's replies that Lorna was being evasive. He got up from the desk where he had remained quietly for a moment once the phone call was finished.

'Thank you, Mrs Graham, you have been most helpful. I don't want you to leave this shop. Open up as usual tomorrow, and let me know if you hear from Mr Challis. You can contact me here.' He handed her a note. 'It's a Crieff number, I'll set off for Perth and hope to see Mr Challis when he returns there. In the meantime, carry on as usual and I'll be back to see you sometime tomorrow. I need to ask you some questions but not before I have seen Mr Challis.'

The inspector said no more and walked out of the shop. In seconds, his car was gone and Jennie was left feeling both mystified and bewildered. She caught sight of Ian putting in the sun-blind and hurried across to him.

He looked at her face and realised it wore a worried frown.

'Whatever is it, Jennie? Is something wrong?'

'I don't know, Ian. I don't understand, but I can't leave the shop. I've been told to stay put.' She started back across the road.

'Wait a minute, Jennie. I'll just lock up and

79

come with you,' he called.

Jennie let him into the shop a few minutes after she'd returned herself.

'Whatever is it, Jennie?' Ian asked her. 'Can you tell me?'

'I've had the police here—' she began to say.

'The police?'

'An inspector from the CID.'

'What did he want?'

Jennie looked up at Ian as though she might hope to find the truth written on his face. Then she shook her head.

'I don't know. He wouldn't tell me anything, only that he was trying to find Adrian.'

Ian sat on the chair next to her and leaned across, taking her hand. Once again, she felt stirred by his touch and was to hold on to him. He gripped her hand firmly as he spoke.

'Listen, Jennie, the CID checks up on all sorts of things. It might be something quite trivial, like a piece of stolen furniture.'

'No, it's not that, Ian. I've had them before looking for stolen things and they tell you straight away what they are looking for. It wasn't like that. He was so serious, almost grim, and only Adrian would do. Do you think he's in some kind of trouble?'

'Jennie, my dear girl, stop worrying. I should think Adrian is more than capable of keeping himself out of mischief. He might be a rogue as far as women are concerned, but he's a good businessman, and you know it.'

She looked at Ian. He was almost willing her to stop worrying and she was sure he was right. She stood up and gave a smile. She had a sudden urge to kiss him and be held in his arms, but his serious gaze kept her crazy impulse in check as she walked with him to the door. She promised to let him know as soon as she had any more news.

She didn't sleep very well that night and went down into the shop next morning half expecting the inspector to be there, waiting for her to open up. But half the day went by and she saw no-one except the occasional customer. Ian popped his head round the door at one point and she managed to reassure him that everything was all right. At lunchtime, she decided to phone Lorna but found her in a strange, worried mood.

'Lorna, it's Jennie. Have you any idea what's going on? Did an Inspector Baillie come to see you?'

A certain strain sounded in Lorna's voice. 'Yes, he did. Adrian wasn't here. Do you know what it's all about, Jennie? Mind you, you'd hardly be ringing to ask me if you knew.'

'No, I don't understand it at all, but I can't help feeling worried for Adrian's sake. What did he say when he came home?'

'He didn't come home.'

'What?' Jennie was unbelieving.

'I waited and waited, but he didn't come. I

don't know where he is, Jennie. I just wish he would turn up. There must be a simple explanation, I am sure. Has the inspector been to see you again, Jennie?'

'No. I've been expecting him all morning but there's been no sign of him.'

Lorna suddenly sounded more positive and practical. 'Jennie, we mustn't worry. There has to be a good explanation and Adrian will explain it all when he turns up. It's up to us to keep the shops going. Are you OK?'

'Yes, Lorna, thank you. I'll keep in touch. Goodbye.'

No sooner had she begun tidying some stock than Inspector Bailie arrived. He made her lock the door, indicating to go into the office. She sat down.

'Mrs Graham, I am assuming that you have had no news of Mr Challis, and I am also assuming that you have been in touch with your colleague in Perth and will know that your employer didn't turn up there last night. Neither has there been any sign of him in Pitlochry or Braemar.' He looked at her searchingly. 'Mrs Graham, I'm going to ask you a single question and it will be easier for you if you give me a direct, honest answer.'

Jennie felt her heart thud.

'Mrs Graham, did you or did you not, on June nineteenth this year, sell to Colonel Robert Fairfax a George Third mahogany chest of drawers for the sum of five and a half thousand pounds?'

'Yes, I did. I'm not sure of the exact date, but I could look it up for you.'

'There's no need. It's obvious you are not lying to me. Having established that, I must ask you to accompany me to Kingowan Police Station for further questioning.'

She stared in terror.

'Did you hear what I said, Mrs Graham?'

Jennie tried to pull herself together. 'Yes, but can I ask why?'

'Not at the moment. Do you need a coat?'

'Well, yes. Would it be all right if I let Mr McWilliam at the bookshop know where I am? He'll wonder why the shop is closing so early.'

'You can phone him.'

She dialled the book-shop number. 'Ian, it's Jennie. Inspector Baillie is here and I have to go to the police station with him for questioning.'

She heard his intake of breath. 'Let me know as soon as you get back, Jennie. It doesn't matter how late.'

She turned to the inspector. 'I'll go upstairs for my coat.'

She found it all beyond her understanding as her thoughts searched for answers during the short journey to the police station. Jennie had never been inside it, but as they entered, she was ushered past the desk sergeant into a small, bare, interview room which held only a table and three chairs. She heard the inspector speak to the sergeant.

'Bring two coffees, please, Sergeant Blakely, and tell Detective Constable Herriott that I am here.' He turned to Jennie. 'Do you take sugar, Mrs Graham?'

'Yes, please.' Her reply was automatic.

A young man had come into the room and the inspector introduced him as Detective Constable Herriott. They all sat down.

In the six hours that followed, Jennie became so tired she could hardly think. The questions were endless and, in between, the inspector made various phone calls and had to wait for replies. Afterwards, she could only remember the questions that really shook her.

She found herself having to go over her whole life in Kingowan, her marriage to Stuart, her work at Moncrieff and Grant, how she had come to be at Kingowan Antiques. And all that without knowing why they were questioning her. Then the awful questions about Adrian.

'How long have you known Mr Challis?' Inspector Baillie asked.

'Since April.'

'You are sure about that?'

'Yes, of course I am sure. Why should I lie?'

He ignored her. 'You had no contact with him when you were working at Moncrieff and Grant?'

'No,' she said shortly, 'I didn't. I've told you all about the time I was working for them.

What is this all about? You haven't told me why I'm here. You haven't told me why you are searching for Adrian and why should I answer all these questions if I don't know what you are trying to get at.'

Incredibly, Inspector Baillie smiled. 'All in good time, Mrs Graham. We just want to try and get the picture first. So you've known Adrian Challis since April. Do you like him? Do you trust him? Is he a good person to work for?'

'I can say yes to all those questions.'

'And socially, Mrs Graham, do you see anything of Mr Challis apart from the time you met him in the shop?'

'I don't think you've any right to ask me that and I'm not going to reply.'

'Very well, I'll put it another way. Does Mr Challis talk to you about his work, about the way the business is run, about his finances, for instance?'

Jennie swallowed hard. Had she been right in thinking that Adrian was in trouble financially when he had been so tetchy about the colonel's cheque? She was careful with her reply.

'He talks about what purchases he has made and a little bit about the other shops. I know nothing of the financial side of the business.'

'And you say you trust him?'

'Yes, I have no reason not to.'

'And you've no idea where he might be at

this moment?'

'No, I haven't.' She almost snapped the words out.

Inspector Baillie said something to his constable who had been making notes all the time Jennie was speaking.

'Right, we'll leave Mr Challis for the time being. Tell me what you know about Colonel Fairfax.'

'Colonel Fairfax?' she repeated stupidly though she knew that his name had been mentioned in the shop.

'Yes, you know him, don't you?'

'Well, yes. Adrian . . . Mr Challis introduced me to him when I first came to the shop. After that, he came in regularly and I got to know him quite well. He is a very nice person who knows a lot about antiques.'

'And when did you last see him?'

'Well, he stopped coming in. I mentioned it to Adrian.'

'Can you say when that happened?'

'Yes, it was after he . . .' She stopped, dismayed.

'Yes, Mrs Graham?'

Jennie found she was stammering.

'It was—it was when—it was after he bought the George Third chest of drawers.' She looked at the inspector, suspicion flooding her mind. 'This is something to do with the chest of drawers, isn't it? You asked me about it in the shop. Was it stolen?'

86

'No, it wasn't stolen, Mrs Graham. This is more serious than theft.'

Jennie was beyond understanding anything. She was tired, weary and even in her distress, she felt empty and hungry.

'What is it?' she whispered.

Inspector Baillie leaned over and picked up a piece of paper from the pile in front of the constable.

'I had a visit from Colonel Robert Fairfax, whom you admit to knowing and to whom you sold the chest of drawers. He was dubious about the authenticity of the piece of furniture and after a few enquiries, he had tests done. It has been proved that the chest is a fake and worth only a few hundred pounds. The colonel paid thousands for it believing it to be genuine.'

Inspector Baillie looked straight at her.

'Mr Adrian Challis was the supplier of the chest and when he can be found, he will be charged with fraud. I have to warn you, Mrs Graham, that if it can be proved that you also knew that the chest was not a genuine piece, then you will be charged also.'

Jennie felt the room spinning, and blackness threatened to overcome her. The inspector moved quickly to thrust her head between her knees, shouting to the constable at the same time, to get some black coffee quickly.

The next thing Jennie knew was that Inspector Baillie was helping her to sit straight in her chair and holding out a cup of coffee to her. She took sips of the strong, sweet liquid and things seemed to return to normal.

'I'm sorry, Mrs Graham, it has been thoughtless of me. You've missed a meal, haven't you? And now you have had a shock. I've sent for some sandwiches for you. Drink your coffee and we won't talk any more for a moment.'

Jennie did as she was told not wanting to think about what had been said to her. She ate her sandwiches and then a policewoman came for the plate and took her through to a small cloakroom. As Jennie looked in the mirror, she hardly recognised herself, her face white, her hair untidy. When was this ordeal going to end or had it only just begun?

When she rejoined the inspector, it was obvious that he and Constable Herriott had also had some coffee and something to eat. They are human after all, she thought ruefully!

'Now, Mrs Graham, it's obvious that the colonel's statement came as a great shock to you. But I will have to question you further. Had you any idea from all your conversations with Mr Challis that there was a possibility that he was dealing in fake pieces of furniture? Or to put it another way, did you believe all the pieces you sold in the shop to be genuine?'

Jennie felt stronger now and quick to jump to Adrian's defence.

'I am quite certain that all the furniture was

genuine, Inspector Baillie. Adrian was a good businessman, with a wide knowledge of antiques. There was never any question of anything being fake or even reproduction. He wouldn't have touched reproduction. He wasn't that kind of dealer, and he worked so hard going to sales and keeping the four shops supplied.'

She stopped and thought for a moment then went on more slowly.

'I'm sure Colonel Fairfax must have made a mistake. Adrian wouldn't have swindled anyone out of such a sum especially a customer he valued as much as Colonel Fairfax. It just doesn't ring true, not any of it.'

'And are you sure that Mr Challis had no financial worries? Did he ever behave in such a way as to make you suspicious? Oh, I seem to have reminded you of something. I think you would be wise to tell me the truth, Mrs Graham.'

Jennie found herself caught off her guard but the sudden memory had come to her of Adrian worrying about the colonel's cheque and then being on edge and uneasy in the weeks that followed.

'It's probably of no significance,' she said at last. 'When I had the cheque from Colonel Fairfax, Adrian told me not to bank it, but came over especially on a Sunday to fetch it.'

'Thank you, Mrs Graham.'

'But, Inspector Baillie, isn't it possible that

89

Adrian himself didn't know the chest was a fake? You seem to be assuming that he had passed off something as genuine and he might have done so in good faith.'

The inspector smiled. 'You earn full marks for loyalty, Mrs Graham, and, of course, you may be right, but there are two things that should remind you of the possibility that he is guilty of fraud. First of all, he is an expert, a professional. If Colonel Fairfax was quick to spot that a piece wasn't genuine then it's unlikely Mr Challis would let it pass through his hands and not recognise it as a fake.

'Secondly, there is his mysterious disappearance. Mrs Stewart at Perth was expecting him and he did not turn up last night. There are many questions to be asked about that. Cast your mind back to my visit yesterday and my departure from Kingowan.' His voice became steely. 'After I had gone, did you telephone Mr Challis anywhere to let him know that I was looking for him?'

Jennie shook her head. 'No, I didn't phone him. Honestly, I don't know where he is and I thought he would be in Perth during the evening.'

'And if you had known where to contact him, would you have warned him?'

She was silent.

'Mrs Graham, please.'

'I don't know,' she said in a small voice, and it was true. She just couldn't think straight.

'Just one more question, Mrs Graham, and then I think I can take you home. It's about Lorna Stewart. How well do you know her and would you trust her?'

Jennie thought of the Lorna she had rather liked, but did she know anything about her? Nothing, not a thing, she said to herself, only that she loves Adrian and had lived with him for a number of years.

'I have asked you about Lorna Stewart, Mrs Graham.' The inspector's voice brought her back.

'I only met her once,' she started to say. 'She seems a nice person.'

'And she lives with Mr Challis but is not his wife?'

'Yes.'

'How did you come to meet her?'

Jennie felt uncomfortable. 'She came to see me.'

'Perhaps she came to warn you off Mr Challis.' Suddenly, the inspector sounded caustic.

'It is none of your business, Inspector Baillie, and has nothing to do with your enquiry,' Jennie replied.

'Everything has something to do with my enquiries and I am very interested in the whereabouts of Mr Adrian Challis. Do you think Mrs Stewart would lie?'

Jennie felt exasperated. 'Really, Inspector Baillie. I've told you I hardly know her. I think you should stick to studying the facts.'

The inspector grinned. 'Touché, Mrs Graham,' and his amiable tone put her off her guard, leaving her unprepared for his next question.

'Mrs Graham, we have talked a lot and you have been co-operative, which is to your advantage. Now, I want a straight answer to one final question.'

She looked into penetrating, blue eyes.

'When you sold that chest of drawers to Colonel Fairfax, did you know it was a fake?'

There was a silence in the small room, broken only by the sound of Constable Herriott writing. Jennie held her breath. She wanted to explode in anger but knew that it would not be wise. She chose her words carefully.

'When I sold the chest of drawers to Colonel Fairfax, I was absolutely certain that it was genuine.'

She felt the inspector's eyes searching her face and when their eyes finally met, she did not waver. The silence was broken by the scrape of a chair as the inspector stood up.

'Thank you, Mrs Graham, that is all. Put on your jacket and I'll take you home. There is no need, I hope, for me to tell you not to repeat to anyone what has gone on between us.'

He saw her expression change and his tone was rather abrupt.

'What is it?'

'It's Ian McWilliam at the bookshop! I promised to let him know when I returned. He knows there's something wrong.'

Inspector Baillie thought for a moment.

'McWilliam? Kingowan Books? Does he know Mr Challis well?'

She nodded. 'I'll take you back to Crieff Road. I'd like to see Mr McWilliam myself. He may be able to help. Then you can speak to him afterwards. I think it might help you to have someone to talk to. It might even jog your memory.'

CHAPTER SEVEN

Jennie watched as the inspector rang the bell at the bookshop before she made her way round the back of the shop to her flat. When she got inside, she sank into a chair without even taking off her jacket. She just sat there, devoid of energy, devoid of feeling, her mind a blank, unable to think or reason or even to remember the hours that had just gone by.

It was nearly eleven o'clock. It would be too late now to see Ian yet he was her only thought. Suddenly, she desperately wanted to see him. She was still sitting there when the bell at the back door rang out shrilly in the silence. Knowing that it must be Ian, she rushed downstairs. As she let him in, she had a hard job to stop herself throwing her arms around him. He looked serious.

'Have you spoken to Inspector Baillie?' she asked him as they went upstairs.

'Yes,' Ian replied gravely. 'He wanted to ask me about Adrian, all sorts of things. Then just as he was leaving, he suddenly became human and told me to come and see you. He thought you needed looking after.'

She faced him across the room and it struck her how handsome he looked in his sweater and casual jeans. He was still looking serious, but his expression had a warmth in it as he held out his arms to her. Jennie was glad to seek their refuge. He held her tight and she felt the tears come to her eyes as she laid her head against his chest.

Then he became practical!

'Let me make you some coffee,' he said. 'Have you had anything to eat at all? You've been gone for hours. I couldn't imagine what it was all about. I was thankful when the inspector came, though I'm none the wiser.'

'I'll make the coffee,' Jennie said. 'It will do me good to do something. I just sat down absolutely exhausted when I got in. I didn't seem to be able to think or feel anything.' Then she remembered. 'I wanted to see you though, Ian. Thanks for coming over.'

She felt better after drinking her coffee.

'It's more than a piece of stolen furniture, isn't it, Jennie?' Ian asked at last.

She nodded. 'I can't talk about it, though the inspector gave me permission to tell you in case you could help. Do you know Colonel Fairfax, Ian?'

'Yes, he sometimes comes into the shop. Doesn't buy much, but likes to have a browse. I know he's been a good customer of Adrian's for years. What has he got to do with all this?'

'I sold him a George the Third chest and it's turned out to be a fake.'

'A fake? Adrian is never dealing in fake stuff?'

'We don't know. You see, he has

95

disappeared!'

Ian looked at her closely. 'Do you feel like telling me the whole story, Jennie, or are you too tired?'

'No, I'd like to talk about it,' she said quietly.

And she proceeded to tell him all that had happened and didn't interrupt.

'So you see, Ian, I am under suspicion, too. It was me who actually sold it to the colonel and took his cheque.'

'Oh, Jennie, you poor girl.' Ian's voice and soft and sympathetic but it quickly changed with his next words. 'But it's Adrian I'm thinking of. His disappearance makes it look as though he's guilty, doesn't it? I would never have believed it possible, though I suppose if he can't be trusted with women then it follows that he can't be trusted with anything.'

Jennie looked troubled.

'We'll just have to hope that Adrian turns up and explains things.' He stood up. 'But, Jennie, it's gone midnight and you must get some sleep. I'll see you tomorrow and you must promise to come over if you are worried.'

She smiled. 'Thank you, Ian. I don't know what I'd do without you.'

The next day, Jennie was on edge, wondering if Adrian would turn up, but she saw no-one except a few customers and a quick visit from Ian. There was no word from Lorna and no sign of the inspector.

By Sunday, she had begun to wonder if she had imagined it all and, for the first time, started to relax a little. When Ian appeared in the middle of the morning, she was pleased to see him and even more pleased at what he had to suggest.

'Come on, young lady,' he said with a smile. 'What are you doing with yourself today? You've had a worrying week and I think you deserve to be taken out for lunch. What do you say? And we could do a bit of hill-walking, too.'

Jennie couldn't get ready quickly enough and eventually joined him in the car with a sigh of satisfaction. They enjoyed a good lunch and the conversation was spent in endless speculation at what Adrian might have done with himself. By the end of the meal, Jennie felt the last of the week's stress disappear and she was delighted when Ian took her for a walk along an uphill moorland road. He pointed to a cluster of stones at the top of a ridge up ahead.

'It's lovely,' she said when they reached the stones and sat down. 'I feel different already, as though this week has never happened.'

'It's nice to be quiet sometimes, isn't it, Jennie?'

She looked at Ian. She was really getting to know him, this Ian McWilliam, and she was sincere when she replied.

'Yes, it is nice to be quiet, Ian, especially

when you are somewhere like this. It's a shame to spoil it with words.'

Jennie could feel the comfort of the silence and she lay back at the foot of the rock and out of the wind. The next thing she knew was a firm hand on her shoulder and Ian's voice calling her name.

'Jennie, Jennie, wake up.'

She opened her eyes to rainy clouds overhead.

'Oh, Ian, I'm sorry. I didn't fall asleep, did I?'

Ian laughed. 'You slept for an hour, Jennie, but don't apologise. You must have needed it. I think we should be making our way down, though, before it gets too cold.'

Jennie got up and stretched herself, 'I do feel a lot better,' she said. 'Thank you for bringing me, Ian. I feel more able to face whatever this week will bring.'

*   *   *

The middle of that week brought Inspector Baillie! Jennie was serving a customer when he came into the shop, but he seemed quite happy to browse and to pretend that he, too, was a customer. When they were alone, he started to walk towards the office. When they were seated, he came straight to the point.

'I take it you've heard nothing from Mr Challis as you haven't contacted me, and Mrs

Stewart hasn't seen him and neither have the people in the Pitlochry or Braemar shops. It would seem that Mr Challis is lying low.'

Jennie frowned. 'He wouldn't—it's not possible that he has gone out of the country, is it?'

'I don't know, Anything is possible, especially as the case has taken a more serious turn.'

She looked at him sharply. 'What do you mean?'

'We've been making enquiries at the other shops and have discovered that the chest sold to Colonel Fairfax was the third of its kind and none of them was a genuine antique. A lot of money is involved and those are the only ones we know about. There could be a lot more.' The inspector was watching Jennie's face. 'You have thought of something, Mrs Graham?'

Jennie hesitated. 'Yes, it's just come back to me. I don't know why I didn't remember it before. When the colonel was looking at the chest, he asked if it was reproduction. Of course, I told him that Adrian didn't deal in reproduction. But what does it all mean? I know there is good reproduction furniture and it's sold at low prices, too, but can some unscrupulous dealers pass it off as genuine? I would have thought that reproduction furniture would have been very easy to spot.'

'It's very interesting, and you are quite right. There are cabinet-makers and small firms who

99

produce nothing but repro, as they call it, and it is sold as such. But, you see, a clever antiques man can touch up a reproduction piece and give it a genuine look. There are all sorts of tricks. Putting on genuine handles, for example, simulating wear and tear. Sometimes it's very difficult to tell the difference.'

'And how did Colonel Fairfax find out?'

'The colonel knew what he was looking for and his suspicions were obviously around in the first place from what you have just said. Apparently, there were tell-tale signs in the chest. For example, the area under the drawer handles should be slightly darker with dirt and grease from handling over the years, but that wasn't so. Then the corners of the drawers, where dirt would have accumulated, were completely fresh and new. Those are the kind of things the expert will look for. It's quite obvious now that the fraud has been going on for a long time and it was only Colonel Fairfax's vigilance that brought it to light.'

He looked at the pretty girl sitting across the desk.

'Mrs Graham, you were under suspicion and we gave you a hard time but I think I can safely say that we can now exclude you from our enquiries. That doesn't mean that we don't still need your help and I want you to promise to get in touch if you learn of anything or remember anything that you might consider suspicious. And there is just one more thing. I

100

shall be sending an expert to each of the shops to look at the pieces of furniture you still have in stock.'

Jennie interrupted. 'You mean I still might have pieces in the shop that are fake? What if I sell them?'

'It will all be done in the next day or so and I will perhaps ask you to look round at the stock yourself. I have given you some guidelines so you know what to look for. You know enough about the business by now to have become quite an expert yourself. I will be on my way now. I've seen Mrs Stewart but I still have to get to Braemar and Pitlochry. Don't be afraid to contact me.'

Jennie saw the inspector out and went back into the shop. A sudden impulse made her pick up the phone to Lorna. They had a quick chat then agreed to meet at a small hotel in a village halfway between Perth and Kingowan. Lorna seemed quite eager to talk.

Jennie set off straight after closing the shop. She realised she hadn't seen Ian that day and didn't know why it should bother her, but she valued Ian's friendship and made up her mind to go and see him first thing the following morning.

Lorna had given her precise instructions to find the hotel and she did so easily. Lorna's car was already parked outside and Jennie found her waiting in the bar. They agreed that they were both hungry and decided to have dinner.

They could chat quietly over their meal and Jennie found that it didn't take Lorna long to mention Inspector Baillie.

'Has the inspector been to see you today, Jennie?'

'Yes, and it wasn't good news, was it? What do you think of it all, Lorna? I cannot believe that Adrian would do anything like that but you have known him for such a long time and you may think differently.'

'I would swear on oath that Adrian wasn't guilty of selling fake furniture. He cares so much about what he deals in, it just isn't like him. Nothing about it rings true,' Lorna said earnestly.

She put down her knife and fork and looked at Jennie across the table.

'And yet, Jennie, there are two things that bother me. You've probably thought of them yourself. First of all, where is he? I haven't heard a word and neither has anyone else. The other thing is personal, but I don't mind telling you. I'm not married to Adrian, as you know, so I've no claim on him, but during the years we've been together, he's been unfaithful more than once and he hasn't always been honest with me. What makes me wonder is if he hid those affairs from me, what else could he possibly be hiding?'

'You know him better than anyone,' Jennie said and abruptly changed the subject. 'Are you supposed to look at the stock in the Perth shop

102

for any more fakes? I was told I had to examine everything closely.'

Lorna nodded. 'Yes, I know, but I'm certain it's all right. I just wish I knew the truth and until Adrian is found, I won't be happy.'

'Do you think any harm could have come to him?'

'No, I don't. He's a survivor and if he's mixed up in this business, he's lying low for some good reason of his own.'

Lorna sounded very positive and Jennie realised how strong a person Lorna really was. They had a lot to discuss about the running of the shop. It was coming up to a quieter time of year, before the Christmas trade picked up, so it did not seem to matter that stocks might run low for a week or two. Surely, Lorna said, the situation couldn't go on like this for very much longer.

Jennie had been glad of the meeting and the talk with Lorna. As she drove home and turned into the back lane that led to her garage behind the shop, she almost ran Ian down in the narrow alley.

'Where on earth have you been?' He demanded. 'I didn't see you all day and then you were missing all evening.'

He's really worried, Jennie thought. It's the first time he has shown any emotion at all, and she felt an unexpected thrill to see him, even if she had upset him.

'I'm sorry, Ian! I agreed to meet Lorna and

rushed off at six o'clock. I was going to come over to see you in the morning.'

She told him of Inspector Baillie's visit and the finding of further fake pieces of furniture. He forgot his irritation in his interest at her news.

'Phew,' he said. 'If Adrian is behind all this, he's been going about it in a big way. No news of him?'

'No, and Lorna hasn't heard from him either. I keep wishing I could just have a word with Adrian to hear what he's got to say. I still find it hard to believe that he could have behaved so dishonestly.'

'Jennie, I want you to promise me that if he does turn up you'll get in touch with me. I want to be there if you are going to talk to him.'

She looked at him wide-eyed. 'But, Ian, surely you don't think there's any harm in Adrian?'

He spoke slowly. 'I don't know, Jennie, I just don't know. All I can say is, be careful.'

He put both hands on her shoulders then, and drew her close to him. He kissed her gently, but briefly. Trying not to show her sense of excitement, Jennie smiled up at him.

'I will be careful, Ian. I promise you I will.'

Another week of tension passed. Every time the shop bell rang, Jennie wondered if it was Adrian or news of Adrian and it was the same if the phone rang. There was also a sense of anti-climax because of the lack of news and the end-of-season feeling in the shop.

Jennie had the expected visit from an antiques expert and she was glad to find that all the furniture in the stock was declared genuine. Lorna phoned every evening, but had little news and Jennie did not see anything of Inspector Baillie.

It was Ian who saved her sanity. Finding her low-spirited, he insisted that they should do something together every evening, even if it was only to have a meal together or a walk by the river.

By the end of the week, Jennie found that she couldn't wait for the evenings and she realised that an hour or two spent in Ian's company was giving her more and more pleasure as she got to know him better. Her feelings baffled her, for Ian behaved like an older brother towards her. She remembered the wild feelings she had felt for Stuart, feelings which had not lasted. She remembered, too, how she had been attracted to Adrian and thought of the concern she still felt for him in spite of his strange behaviour.

But with Ian, it was different. She found herself longing for the touch that never came; she listened, in vain, for any words of endearment or any expression that might give a hint to his own feelings. She was sure she was coming to love him but was it possible, she asked herself, to love a man just because he was kind and caring?

When she was with him, she had no difficulty in hiding her feelings. When she was away from him, she thought of him most of the time. She had one precious memory which she treasured. It was the brief kiss he had given her on the night she had met Lorna and found him so anxious. There had been no meaning behind the caress, but she hugged the thought of it to herself and it gave her hope.

When Saturday morning came, she gave up hope of seeing anything of Inspector Baillie and was looking forward to the next day when she and Ian had planned a day's walking. The shop had been open only ten minutes, however, when the inspector appeared. He greeted her with a smile and she knew straight away that there was no news. It must be a routine visit.

'How have you got on this week, Mrs Graham? I hear that an expert from Sotheby's came to see you.'

She nodded. 'Yes, he didn't find anything, but what about the other shops? Am I allowed to ask you?'

'Just a set of small tables at Pitlochry. They had been in the shop for some time and young Jonathan Crocker there had no idea that they were fake. But that brings me to a question I have to ask you. Jonathan has known Adrian for several years and is very shocked at the whole business. Like you, he is unwilling to believe that Adrian is capable of such a fraud. But I got him talking about Adrian and, delving into his memory, a name has come up. I want to ask you, Mrs Graham, if you know anything of a John McKenzie.'

Jennie looked at the inspector, very puzzled. There can't be any connection, she thought, but I have to be honest.

'Well, yes, I do,' she replied. 'I know John very well indeed. He's a friend of my father's. They went to school together. But why do you ask? The John McKenzie I know couldn't possibly have any connection with Adrian. He's a schoolmaster.'

Inspector Baillie looked at her, realising this girl was not capable of untruthfulness or evasion.

'He has no connection with the furniture or cabinetmaker's business?'

'No, none at all. He teaches physics. What is it, inspector? Have you been given a lead?'

'I don't know. Jonathan can remember Adrian once rushing off in a hurry because he had to see a John McKenzie. The name slipped out just like that and Jonathan doesn't really know why he remembered it.'

Jennie was inclined to scorn. 'But that is ridiculous. It doesn't mean anything, and there must be hundreds of John McKenzies.'

The inspector took her up quickly. 'You don't know my job, my dear. The slightest scrap of information can often provide the biggest clue. I'll go to Perth. Mrs Stewart may be able to help. If you see McWilliam, would you ask him if the name means anything to him?'

No sooner had the inspector's car disappeared than Ian was in the shop.

'I mustn't stop a minute,' he said, 'but I recognised Inspector Baillie's car. Is there any news?'

Jennie went up to him, conscious of his height, his dark hair, his good looks, and, as always, his serious expression.

'He said I was to ask you if you knew of a John McKenzie in connection with Adrian.'

'John McKenzie?' Ian shook his head. 'It's a common enough name, and I daresay I have known a John McKenzie in my time, but certainly nothing to do with Adrian. Is that all the inspector wanted?'

'Yes. He doesn't seem to be getting anywhere.'

'Oh, well, we've both got shops to run. I'll try to forget Adrian Challis for the time being and hope you will, too.'

Jennie watched him walk back across the road and disappear into the bookshop. Oh, Ian, she thought and set about busying herself so that she would forget both Ian and Adrian.

Half-an-hour later that morning, Jennie had finished some dusting and decided, while it was still quiet, to tidy a pile of brochures and catalogues of sales and auctions which Adrian had collected over the years, for reference.

I'll put them in alphabetical order, she said to herself. It'll make it easier for Adrian when he is looking for something. Amongst them, she found a brochure about the Braemar shop, and because she, had never been there, she flipped through it. As she did so, a small card fell out. She picked it up and read the few words that were printed on it. As she did so, her heart nearly stopped beating, for on the card were printed the words: John McKenzie, Cabinetmaker, Bhreac Cottage, Invermuir, Near Braemar.

CHAPTER EIGHT

Jennie said the name over and over again to herself as she stared at the card in her hand. John McKenzie, Cabinetmaker—he must be the one. Would he know where Adrian was?

She felt a surge of uninhibited excitement go through her. Here's my chance to do something, she said to herself. I'll go and see him and tell the inspector afterwards. I can be up there in the time it would take to get a message to Inspector Baillie. Jennie tried to quell her tumultuous thoughts and set herself to do things in a logical order. Lock up the shop, run upstairs and get her anorak, find the road map . . .

As she secured the lock, she remembered about Ian. Should I tell him, she wondered. It would be sensible, but he might object and try and stop me.

It was when she found the road map that she realised she would have to tell Ian, for she needed help. She knew where Braemar was, but looked in vain for Invermuir. She needed a large-scale map and would have to get one from Ian.

She ran across the road and had a quick feeling of relief when she realised he was on his own.

'Jennie!' A rare smile came into his eyes

when he saw her but it soon changed to a frown. 'What is it? You're up to something! I know by your face.'

'Ian, have you got a large-scale map of the Braemar district?'

He didn't say anything but reached for a map and opened it out for her. She found the spot immediately and also found Invermuir nestling at the top of a small glen.

'Oh, Ian, it's all so exciting. Look what I've found.' She handed him the card. 'It must be the same John McKenzie, don't you think?'

He nodded slowly. 'It looks like it, but where did you find it?'

'In a brochure. I was having a tidy up and it just fell out.'

'Have you phoned Inspector Baillie?'

It was the question Jennie had been dreading and she didn't answer immediately.

'Jennie?' Ian asked, a note of sharpness in his voice.

'I know you'll say I'm not to do it, but I'm going to. I can get there as quickly as I can tell the inspector. He could be anywhere. I'll be able to ask this John McKenzie if he knows anything about Adrian.'

She found her arm held in a vice-like grip.

'Jennie, you are not to go. You'd be a fool! It's a shot in the dark in any case and it's asking for trouble.'

She looked at him in astonishment.

'Whatever do you mean? I'm only going to

111

ask the man a few questions. I'll be back by tea-time and I'll phone the inspector then.' She pulled her arm away. 'You can't stop me, Ian. I'm fed-up being stuck in the shop waiting for news and wondering all the time what's going on. This is the first, real clue we've had.'

'Yes, and it shouldn't be you who's following it up.'

'Well, I've made up my mind and I'm going. It's not that far and I know the way now. I'll come and tell you how I get on as soon as I get back.'

'Jennie . . .'

But Jennie was already out of the shop and hurrying down the back lane to fetch her car. She'd soon left Kingowan behind and made good time as she headed for Braemar. Finding the glen she was looking for wasn't difficult, and her heart leaped when she saw the sign for Invermuir.

The tiny village was no more than a huddle of cottages on a steep hillside, so she had no trouble in finding Bhreac Cottage. With its name on the gate, the low, whitewashed, stone cottage was hidden in trees down a short path.

For the first time since she had left Kingowan, Jennie felt nervous. This was such an isolated place and she didn't know anything about this John McKenzie! Jennie knocked at the door, using the heavy, metal knocker.

The sound seemed to echo through the trees behind the building. When there was no

112

sound from within, she knocked again. There must be someone here, she thought. I can't have come all this way to find no-one at home! If he's a cabinetmaker, surely he must work here.

She didn't know how long she stood there before she began to look around. The small garden was completely overgrown; thistles choked the lawn and the path was almost green with moss and grass. There were curtains at the windows, half-drawn, but looking shabby. Suddenly, she felt very uneasy.

I'll just try the door and if it's locked, I'll have to go, she decided.

The round door handle turned easily and suddenly, Jennie found the door open. She stepped inside, into a long room and immediately realised, in amazement, that there was a strong smell of cooking food greeting her. Jennie plucked up courage.

'Mr McKenzie?' she called out as loudly as she dared. 'Are you there?'

She heard a sound from the back, obviously the kitchen, then a door at the end opened and a man stepped into the room.

'Who is it?'

Jennie gasped and stood rooted to the spot. She couldn't be sure at first, for the man's hair was long and his face dark with several days' growth of beard. But as he stepped out of the shadows, her first suspicions were confirmed— it was Adrian!

'What on earth are you doing here?' he burst out in anger. 'How did you find me, Jennie Graham?'

Jennie tried not to show that she was frightened, but this was not the Adrian she had known, not the Adrian of the charm and winning ways.

'I didn't expect to find you, Adrian. I came looking for John McKenzie. Is he here?'

A short bark of laughter came back at her and she felt the sweat of fear in her hands.

'No, he's not! And now that you are, what are we going to do about that then?' Adrian sneered.

He had walked the length of the room towards Jennie then sat down at a small table beside the fireplace. It was piled with books and papers.

'Sit down, Jennie, sit down. We might as well have a chat now that you are here and you can tell me what's happening.'

Jennie sat down thankfully, feeling as though her legs would no longer hold her up.

'I have to know the truth, Adrian, about you! Did you fake the furniture?'

'And how much does dear Jennie know about it all? You'd better tell me the truth, and you'd better tell me where this Inspector Baillie fits into it, too.'

She looked at the evil expression on his face and felt like creeping away again, back to Kingowan, but curiosity suddenly got the better of her.

'How did you know about Inspector Baillie?' she asked.

'Lorna told me.'

'Lorna!'

'Yes! She's a good girl. Phoned me at Braemar to tell me about Inspector Baillie so I didn't go home that night. I haven't been home since, in fact.'

'And does she know about the fakes?'

'No, not Lorna. I kept it to myself.' He laughed suddenly. 'You can't believe it, can you, Jennie, innocent Jennie? I fell for you, you know. I really meant that. But it all went wrong! Did Colonel Fairfax go to the police?'

'Yes, he did and they've been hunting everywhere for you, They found other fakes, too, from years ago. Does Mr McKenzie make them?'

'Johnny? Johnny doesn't make anything. He's been dead for five years! Had a good business making reproduction, he did, and I've been working on his leftovers. Now I've got you curious, haven't I? There's a lot you don't know about me, Jennie Graham.'

He sat forward in his chair.

'You didn't know I was a dab hand at making reproduction look like the genuine article, did you? Fetched thousands instead of hundreds they did. But I didn't deceive the dear, old colonel. They say that every criminal makes a mistake one day and that was mine. It was my most ambitious piece, a George the Third chest that would take in even Colonel Fairfax, but I went wrong somewhere. Do you know where I went wrong, Jennie? It's a matter of professional pride, so don't be afraid to tell me.'

'Something about the dark areas under the handles and in the corners of the drawers,' she whispered.

'Blast! I didn't think he'd notice that. Are you sure you didn't help to make him suspicious?'

'Me?' Her voice was raised into a thin screech. 'What have I got to do with it, Adrian Challis? It was bad enough being a suspect to begin with. Six hours they kept me at the police station. But why, that's what I don't understand. Why, Adrian? You had a successful business, you can't have needed the money . . .'

'Not need the money! Everyone needs money.' His expression was nasty. 'But it wasn't just the money. I liked being clever enough to deceive people, and I succeeded. I deceived Lorna, too, but she always forgave me. Good, old Lorna.'

'You are really wicked, aren't you?' Jennie said as she looked at his drawn, twisted face. 'But you've had it now the hunt is on for you.'

'Whom did you tell?' he snapped out suddenly. 'Does the inspector know about Johnny's address?'

Jennie altered. 'No,' she said in a small voice, 'I'm on my own.'

The laughter rang out again. 'So, no-one knows where you are or where I am. That's good, little Jennie, that's good. I can make sure you don't tell anyone and then I can make my getaway. It's sooner than I planned, but no matter.'

'What do you mean, Adrian?'

'No harm in telling you. I haven't been here all the time. I went straight to London and sold the business. Had a friend who's been pestering me to sell it to him. He came up and looked round the Perth shop and made me a good offer. I'm just waiting for the money to come through, then I shall go abroad—South America, where they can't touch me. Have a fancy to take Lorna with me. Do you think she would come?'

Jennie couldn't say anything. She tried to think clearly. What if Adrian did tie her up and got away? Ian would soon find her. But why should he get away with it, she was thinking. She ought to try and get the truth back to Inspector Baillie.

'No reply, Jennie?' came the hard, taunting voice. 'Thinking of how you are going to escape from me and let the dear inspector know, I expect.'

Jennie knew she would have to act quickly, and her mind was racing ahead. She would pretend stupidity and then make a dash for

117

it . . .

'I wouldn't tell the inspector, Adrian. I came here looking for Mr McKenzie to see if I could help you.'

'And you still want to help me after what I've told you?'

'I wouldn't like to see you in prison, Adrian.'

He laughed quietly then and she saw her opportunity. She got up quickly and turned towards the door.

'I promise I won't say anything, Adrian . . .'

'Stay where you are.'

The words were barked out and she froze where she was, at the same time turning to face him. He had risen, walked round the table and was pointing a gun at her! Fear seemed to hit Jennie in a ridiculous reaction—she laughed in his face.

'I imagine that's one of your fakes, Adrian Challis.'

There was a deafening report as Jennie saw that the gun had been pointed to the ceiling and fired. At exactly the same time, there was an equally deafening noise as the front door burst open. She felt like cheering as she heard Ian's voice.

'Lie flat, Jennie.'

And then she was thrown to the floor! She sensed that Adrian had moved quickly and was about to fire again.

'Ian!' she screamed out.

But Adrian misfired and the bullet bedded itself in the wall behind Ian's shoulder. At the same time, Ian threw himself in a rugby tackle, catching Adrian by the legs. The gun clattered to the floor and Jennie, without thinking, picked it up and slipped it into her pocket.

The two men were fighting and struggling now, but Adrian was no match for the tall, athletic Ian who had suddenly become a fighting fury. The blows to Adrian's head made him sag and one crushing, final hit from Ian sent Adrian crashing down. He hit his head on the brick fireplace and lay still.

'Run for it, Jennie,' Ian gasped out. 'Where's the gun?'

'I've got it.'

In seconds, they were down the front path and into Ian's car, parked across the gateway. They were both out of breath and said nothing as Ian revved up the engine and sped off down the narrow lane. She felt him glance down at her and automatically prepared herself for his angry outburst.

All she wanted at that moment was comfort, the comfort of his arms around her, her name on his lips. But she knew she didn't deserve these things. She had risked her own life and his.

'I hope you're satisfied with your meddling, young lady. You wouldn't listen to me, would you?' he said eventually.

'Ian—'

'No, you are going to listen to me now. Don't you ever dare behave like that again! Rushing off into danger without a thought to your own safety. You're nothing but a little fool—'

Jennie couldn't speak for the lump in her throat and she could feel tears trickling down her cheeks. She gave a sob.

'Jennie . . .'

She didn't move as he slammed on the brakes and pulled up at the side of the road. In an instant, she was in his arms, safe and secure. She was aware of his lips coming down on her mouth gently and they sat together in silence, but only for a few minutes. He pushed her away gently and started up the car again.

'We'll go to the police station in Pitlochry, as fast as we can and try to get in touch with Inspector Baillie.'

Jennie sat beside him, her heart singing with joy. He had held her in his arms and he had kissed her! That was all that seemed to matter at that moment.

It was mid-afternoon when they pulled into the police station. As Ian helped her out of the car, he noticed the bulge in her anorak pocket.

'What's that?' he asked abruptly. 'What's that in your pocket?'

She had quite forgotten she was carrying a gun!

'It's Adrian's gun,' she whispered.

'Don't touch it.'

He took a handkerchief from his own pocket and wrapped it carefully round the gun and carried it into the police station. Jennie followed. It took Ian no more than a few minutes to explain the situation clearly and Inspector Baillie was contacted on his car phone. Jennie listened to the conversation.

'Yes. Ian McWilliam here. We've found Adrian Challis, inspector . . . near Braemar . . . oh, you're in Braemar yourself? Well, take the road up the glen to Invermuir. It's Bhreac Cottage. Mrs Graham's car is standing outside. You can't miss it.'

Jennie couldn't make out what the inspector was saying before Ian continued.

'I don't know, he could be, but he was unconscious when we left him. I might have killed him for all I know . . . yes, we've got one gun here, but it doesn't mean to say that he hasn't got another . . . Stay here? Yes, we will. Goodbye.'

Ian turned and looked at Jennie as he put down the phone.

'It looks as though the inspector was on the same trail. He was at Braemar.' He turned to the desk sergeant and gave him the gun. 'You'd better have charge of this, and is there anywhere we can wash and have something to eat? We'd like to stay here until the inspector arrives.'

'There's only one of the cells, sir, but you're welcome to have some chairs in there and I

121

could send out for sandwiches. There's a wash-basin in the cell and I'll get you a towel.'

Ian thanked him and turned to Jennie, grinning.

'Fancy having lunch in a police cell with me, Jennie?' he asked.

'Ian, how can you joke about it?'

'I don't know, really. It must be a reaction. If you can cry, why can't I laugh?'

'Oh, Ian.'

They sat side by side on the bed in the cell while the sergeant brought them coffee and some rather dry-looking sandwiches. Jennie drank her coffee and ate her sandwiches and began to feel better. She knew she was in for a lecture from Ian and she knew she deserved it.

'Ian, I just don't understand how you came to burst in the door just as that moment,' she said hesitantly.

He was silent for a short while.

'We've got to go further back than that, Jennie. I was very, very angry with you and also very anxious, too.'

'But why, Ian? I was only going to see a cabinetmaker. Why did you think there was any harm in going in the first place?'

'I don't know. I just had a sense of danger, call it a sixth sense if you like. I am a Scot after all! But I think it must have been aroused because I was so sensitive about your safety. I was terrified you would come to some harm.'

Jennie let his words sink in, words she

thrilled to hear.

'So what did you do?' she asked him.

'As soon as you had run out of the shop, I shut up shop. I had seen the address on the card you showed me and you had more or less pointed it out on the map, so I followed you. I knew you were on such a high that you would never notice me. I arrived at Bhreac Cottage just as you went into the house so I knew—or thought I knew—that you'd found John McKenzie at home.'

'There was no reply when I knocked at the door so I opened it and went in,' Jennie said. 'I've never been so shocked in my life as when I found Adrian there. What did you do then?'

'First of all, I waited in the car, but I was uneasy. I had a good chance to look around and could see how rundown the place was. You didn't come out so I decided to creep up to the house. From under the window I could hear voices and thought all was well. Then, I don't know, something made me suspicious and I moved to the door. That was when I got my shock, for I realised that it was Adrian you were talking to, and it sounded like Adrian in an ugly mood.'

Ian stopped talking and put an arm round Jennie.

'I'm sorry, Jennie, that's when I made the mistake. I should have made myself known straight away but I didn't trust Adrian so I waited. I didn't know he had a gun until I heard it go off, and you know the rest.'

'But, Ian, you went for him when he still had the gun in his hand.'

'I didn't seem to think about it. I only thought of you in danger and the rugby tackle was a reflex action. I had to silence him somehow and it wasn't difficult.'

'Ian, you saved my life.'

'I don't know about that, Jennie. We shall never know, but you are safe and that is the most important thing. But what happened, Jennie? Wasn't John McKenzie there?'

Jennie told him what Adrian had told her about John McKenzie and the reproduction furniture and how it was Adrian's intention to escape to South American and take Lorna with him.

'There's something you haven't thought of, Jennie. When I knocked Adrian down, he banged his head on the fireplace. He was out cold. He might not have got up again.'

'You mean you might have killed him?'

'It's a possibility,' he said soberly.

'It was self-defence,' she said stoutly. 'We've got the gun to prove it and the bullet holes.'

'You would stick up for me then?' She could tell he was smiling.

'Of course I would, even if you are cross with me.'

'I daresay I'll forgive you, now it's all over, but it was a foolish thing to do, Jennie.'

'But, Ian, how was I to know that I was

going to find Adrian there? And that he would have a gun. I'm a Scot, too, but I haven't got sixth sense.'

She sat in silence for a moment. The ordeal was over and she was revelling in the new-found Ian. He had dropped so many little hints to give her cause to think that he cared for her and she knew now that she loved him. She felt she could have shouted it aloud but a police cell was hardly the place.

While they waited for the inspector, Jennie told Ian all that Adrian had said and it was in the middle of this conversation that Inspector Baillie arrived, certainly not looking pleased with the pair of them!

'Here you are, and a good place for the two of you, in a police cell. You thought you'd take the law into your own hands, did you?'

Jennie looked at him, her heart sinking. It sounded like bad news.

'Adrian, Inspector Baillie,' she asked in a nervous voice. 'Did you find him alive?'

The inspector looked grim.

'I didn't find him at all,' he said. 'He had disappeared.'

CHAPTER NINE

Ian and Jennie looked at each other, both knowing that the other was thinking that at least Adrian was alive. Inspector Baillie's voice interrupted their thoughts.

'You had better come into the office, to take your statements. By the way, Mrs Graham, Constable Herriott has driven your car back. You'd left your keys in the ignition.'

Jennie was tempted to giggle and didn't dare look at Ian as they followed the inspector into a large office where he ordered tea.

'And which of you started this fiasco?' he then asked.

Jennie knew she must be the first to speak and told of how she had found John McKenzie's card.

'But why didn't you let me know?' he thundered at her.

'That's what Ian said,' she whispered shakily. 'I just thought I'd go and find this Mr McKenzie and phone you afterwards.'

'And presumably Mr McWilliam followed you on this madcap scheme.'

'Yes,' Ian replied. 'I was very angry with her, but couldn't stop her. She was running for her car before I had time to lock up the shop. She didn't know it but I didn't let her out of my sight.'

'And now, tell me again what happened at Mr McKenzie's cottage.'

Between them, they told the whole story and everything that Adrian had said. It took a few hours and it was getting dark before they finished.

'Where do you think Adrian is now? Will he be able to get away to South America like he said?' Jennie asked as their account came to an end.

'He will not, God willing,' the inspector said grimly. 'You'd better hear my side of the story and just how much you interfered in the course of justice. Through our computer system, we had discovered the whereabouts of John McKenzie, cabinetmaker, also that he had died five years ago. When your call came through, we were actually in Braemar and on our way to investigate. Had we got there first, we could have arrested Adrian Challis and saved ourselves a lot of trouble, not to mention putting people in danger.

'When we did reach the cottage, your car was still there, Mrs Graham, but there was no sign of Challis. I did, however, find a note on the table. It said, 'Hi, Inspector, just off to South America. Sorry to miss you.' '

Jennie could sense the inspector's displeasure.

'You see,' he continued, 'he had guessed how long it would take you to contact me and for me to get to Braemar, but he had reckoned without two things—the fact that I was already on my way and the car telephone. With the use of that phone, I was immediately able to contact our headquarters and put a call out to all airports to stop Mr Challis from flying out of the country. I knew he couldn't use a false name because of his passport.'

He stopped, looking weary. 'I have to wait for a call now. I suggest that you two get yourselves to the nearest hotel and try to get a good night's sleep. I shall need you here first thing in the morning.'

Ian and Jennie not only found a hotel, but a hotel willing to produce a supper for them at nine-thirty in the evening. They sat alone in the small dining-room, but Jennie felt she hardly had the energy to eat.

'Come on,' Ian urged. 'You'll sleep better if you've had something to eat.'

'I just feel so foolish,' she said. 'I must have been mad to rush off like that. I wouldn't listen to you, would I?'

'Stop worrying and start eating,' he ordered. 'The sooner you get to bed, the better. You will feel differently in the morning.'

Their rooms were on different floors so Jennie said good-night to Ian on the first landing.

'Thanks, Ian, for coming to my rescue. I'll never forget it.'

Laughingly, he drew her into his arms. She was glad to feel so close to him.

'I shan't forget in a hurry either,' he said.

'Look at me, Jennie.'

She raised her head, to see a softness in his expression. She reached up to meet his lips in a long, searching kiss which brought a weakness to her limbs and a desire to stay in his arms for ever.

'Sleep well, Jennie,' was all he said as they drew apart. 'Good-night.'

'Good-night, Ian.'

Jennie stumbled into bed and her last thoughts were not of the violence of earlier in the day but of Ian's kiss.

'Oh, Ian,' she murmured as she fell asleep . . .

They had breakfast together in good spirits, both of them revived by the night's rest.

'How long do you think Inspector Baillie will keep us here?' Jennie asked.

'I've no idea,' Ian replied. 'There's not a lot more we can do and I'm anxious to get back to the shop. I know it's Sunday, but I've got some boxes of books to unpack and price and put out for tomorrow. I don't want to lose another day.'

At eleven o'clock, a tired, dishevelled inspector arrived.

'It's all right for some,' he grumbled. 'You didn't have to be up all night waiting for reports from the airports.'

'Have you any news?' Jennie asked.

'No,' he snapped. 'Nothing at all. He's vanished. He's either lying low or he's slipped through our fingers. I've had officers looking for him at Perth but there's no sign of him or Mrs Stewart. Their house is locked up and neighbours report seeing them in a car yesterday afternoon.'

He looked at them both.

'I don't suppose there's anything you can say to help, so there's no point in keeping you here. You get back to Kingowan and I'll keep in touch with you there. If we catch him, you realise that it will be a court case and you'll have to give evidence. Apart from the fraud, we've now got possession of firearms and attempted murder to consider. Fortunately, no-one has come to any harm.'

Jennie and Ian said goodbye to him in the carpark and each drove off in their own cars.

As she drove along, Jennie had mixed feelings. She thought of Ian and Adrian equally, both of whom she had seen in a different light in the past twenty-four hours. If Adrian and Lorna had managed to get away to South America, in one way it would be a relief, as the law couldn't touch them there and she would not be involved in any court case.

On the other hand, Adrian had defrauded several people and had used threatening behaviour towards her. If Ian hadn't arrived when he did, anything could have happened. A voice of reason told her that it was not right that Adrian should go free and she steeled herself to face up to court proceedings once again.

The thoughts about Adrian were interspersed with the memory of Ian's behaviour. He had risked an attack on himself to protect her and had been more than caring. He had been almost loving. But did he love her, she asked herself.

He had kissed her with passion, but no words of love had passed between them. She would have to be patient . . .

That patience was sorely tried during the next week. Jennie opened the shop and continued to serve her customers from the dwindling stock. She saw nothing of Inspector Baillie and her only contact with Ian was a wave and a greeting from across the road at opening and closing times. What she had expected, she didn't know, but it certainly hadn't been a flat, boring nothingness.

By the end of that week, she had almost decided that she would give up in Kingowan and return to Edinburgh where she could find a secretarial job. The months in the antique shop and in the flat had served her well, but now that Stuart was completely out of her life, she felt she should make a new start.

She had to admit to herself a total disappointment as far as Ian was concerned. She'd thought she had become so close to him over the week-end, believing she had seen a glimpse of an Ian totally different from the sober, respectable, bachelor bookseller.

I must have got things out of proportion,

she said to herself, reading into his words something that just did not exist.

In the first post on the Friday, there was a letter from a Lester Harrington, to tell her he was now the owner of Kingowan Antiques and that he proposed to visit her on the morning of Friday, October second to look round and to give her his proposals for the shop.

Jennie rushed to the calendar.

'That's today!' she shouted aloud. 'Any minute! I must tidy up.'

She got out the duster and flew round, tidied the office and had a quick look at the flat in case he wanted to see it, too. An hour later, he arrived.

He was a tall, powerfully-built man who almost filled the doorway. Although his hair was grey, he looked nowhere near even middle-age.

'Mrs Graham? Lester Harrington, pleased to meet you. I've bought the business from Adrian—been after it a long time, wanted to expand into Scotland. I hear the old rascal has gone to South America. He was looking tired last time I saw him.'

Jennie listened to him with a growing sense of amazement. It was obvious that Mr Harrington knew nothing of Adrian's false dealings and she thought it was not her place to say anything.

He was looking around him.

'Yes, Adrian said it was small, but it will suit

my purpose. May I have a look upstairs? I understand there's a flat. Is it occupied?'

'Yes, I am living in it.'

'I see.'

He was gone only a few minutes.

'Excellent, excellent,' he said. 'And this is the office. Yes, that could easily be moved upstairs. Sit down, Mrs Graham. I'm afraid I have some news for you that you may not like. I don't suppose Adrian gave you any warning, as it was all signed up in such a rush.'

Jennie looked at him. No nonsense about this man. He knew what he wanted and she had an uncomfortable feeling he wasn't going to want her.

'I plan to enlarge the shop, Mrs Graham. The office can be taken from the ground-floor selling space and moved upstairs. I intend to knock the flat into a showroom for the sale of reproduction furniture. I know that Adrian has always made a point of sticking to genuine antiques, but they are pricey, and it is my experience that there is a good market for high-class reproductions. I have a good supplier.'

He looked across at Jennie.

'So I am sorry to have to tell you that I will have to give you a month's notice to leave. However, I'd like to pay you a month's salary, but ask you to leave sooner so that I can get the building work in hand.'

Jennie gulped. True, she had been thinking

of leaving and moving to Edinburgh, but to find herself suddenly without a home was a different matter!

'When do you want me to go, Mr Harrington?' she asked nervously.

'Shall we say the end of the week? Will that give you enough time to make alternative arrangements?'

She had to agree. It was out of her hands.

As he went out of the door, Inspector Baillie walked in, looking behind him at the tall, disappearing figure.

'Good-morning, Mrs Graham. Was that one of your customers?'

'No, it was the new owner. I told you that Mr Challis had sold out.'

'So you did. I wouldn't mind having a word with that gentleman,' he said thoughtfully.

'Inspector, Adrian told him he was going to South America, but I swear he didn't know anything about the fraud.'

'Let's go and sit down, young lady. You don't need to lock up.'

'Have you any news?'

'Yes and no. Mr Adrian Challis has certainly kept us busy.'

They sat down in the office.

'First of all,' he said, 'I have to tell you that I have received no reports of a Mr Challis flying out from any of the main airports. We concentrated on Edinburgh and went through all the lists of departures for that Saturday.

No-one by the name of Challis, but on the other hand, a Mr and Mrs Stewart took a standby flight to Heathrow at six o'clock that evening. We managed to get a description of the couple.

'Then we switched our enquiries to Heathrow. Sure enough, a Mr and Mrs Stewart got on a flight for South America early on Sunday morning having stayed the night at one of the airport hotels. However, we lost them. I am very sorry, but we lost them, and we can't touch them in South America. We had final proof of our investigations this week. A car left standing in the airport carpark at Edinburgh proved to belong to Mr Challis.' The inspector looked across at Jennie. 'What are you thinking, Mrs Graham?'

'I don't know,' she stammered. 'I can't take it in. If they went as Mr and Mrs Stewart, then Adrian must have got hold of a false passport. His passport would have to be in the name of Stewart, wouldn't it?'

'Precisely. Our Mr Challis obviously knew where to go for a passport while he was in London. He was a slippery customer, Mrs Graham, and you have come out of it very lightly. I am sorry we didn't catch him. I would have like to have seen him in dock.'

'And you would have caught him if it hadn't been for me.'

'That we shall never know for sure, and I hope that you can put the episode behind you.

Are you staying on here at the shop?'

Jennie shook her head. 'No, Mr Harrington has just told me that he is altering the premises and wants the flat for a showroom. He's going to sell reproduction furniture.'

She managed to grin at the idea and the inspector laughed also.

'Very appropriate. Perhaps now we shall have no more trouble from Kingowan Antiques. By the way, Mr Challis sold his house in Perth weeks ago. I think he must have sensed that he'd gone too far when he sold that chest to Colonel Fairfax. I'll have to visit the colonel and tell him his villain has got away with it. In fact, I'll go out there next.' He shook hands with Jennie.

'Goodbye, Mrs Graham, and please, don't go chasing any more criminals!'

'I won't! Goodbye.'

Jennie sat down somewhat bemused after he had left. Her world had turned upside down in one, quick hour. Adrian was out of her life and she'd no job, though she would be all right financially for a few weeks. But she'd nowhere to live, unless she went home again. It all pointed to a visit to Edinburgh to look around.

And Ian? She would have to forget Ian. She knew he was a person she could love very dearly but she would have to face up to the fact that he wasn't for her.

The phone ringing broke into her thoughts.

'Kingowan Antiques,' she answered

automatically.

'Jennie.'

It was Ian! She couldn't believe it, just when she had been thinking of him.

'Hello, Ian.'

'Jennie, was that Inspector Baillie? Is there any news?'

'Yes, lots of news.'

'I can't come over now, but what about meeting me tonight? Come for a walk along the river. Eight o'clock?'

'Ian, it'll be dark!'

'Blast, of course it will! Come over for a drink then. I must see you. Must go. See you later.'

When the evening came, Jennie felt quite excited, but knew that she must try to hide her feelings. She dressed carefully in a bright, woollen skirt and a soft, blue sweater that deepened the colour of her eyes.

Ian let her in and seemed pleased to see her.

'I've opened a bottle of wine, Jennie. I don't know what we've got to celebrate but at least the anxieties of last week-end are over.'

Upstairs, in the gracious, long living-room, the curtains were drawn and two lamps provided a soft glow of light over everything.

'And what did the inspector have to say?' Ian asked her as he poured two glasses of wine.

When Jennie told him the story, Ian gave a low whistle.

'He was quite a lad, Adrian, wasn't he? He's got away with it but, in a way, I'm glad there's not going to be a court case.'

Jennie nodded. 'Yes, it is a relief.'

'Did you care for him a lot, Jennie?'

She stared at him. Surely he didn't think there had been something going on between herself and Adrian?

'No, I didn't, not at all. I found him attractive, but that's a different matter.'

'But it was more than that to Adrian?' Ian was persistent.

She laughed. 'He asked me to marry him, if you must know. Said he would leave Lorna, but I didn't take him seriously.'

'I thought from the way you were rushing off to warn him that you must be attached to him in some way.'

'Good heavens, no. I certainly gave you the wrong impression if you thought that. He's best forgotten now. And I haven't told you all that has happened yet.'

Ian groaned. 'Not further trouble, I hope.'

Jennie smiled. 'Well, it is in a way but I daresay it will work out all right. I had a visit from Mr Harrington this morning, the new owner of Kingowan Antiques. He has bought Adrian out. He's going to enlarge the shop, turn the flat into a showroom and he's given me the sack!'

'Jennie!'

'Well, that's exaggerating, I suppose. He's

138

paid me a month's salary and asked me to leave next week.'

She could see concern in Ian's face and thought she must be imagining it, but there was also a hint of relief.

'And what are you going to do, Jennie?'

She took the plunge. 'I am closing the shop one day day next week and going down to Edinburgh to look for a flat and to find out what the job situation is like.'

'You don't mind going back to Edinburgh?'

'I have no choice. Stuart and all the troubles I had there are a thing of the past. I've got to think of the future.'

Jennie was trying to sound sensible, but she felt as though her heart was breaking and she could feel an inner tremble as she awaited Ian's reaction. It came with a force that shook her.

'You are not going back to Edinburgh, Jennie.'

'Ian!' The protest in her voice was because he had got up, pulled her to her feet and had taken her into his arms.

'Jennie, you are not going to Edinburgh,' he repeated, and then kissed her.

Jennie felt herself go limp in his arms. Then she was caught tightly against him and he was saying all the things she had wanted to hear for a long time.

'You are not going to Edinburgh or anywhere else. You are staying here in

139

Kingowan and you are going to marry me and live in this very house.'

'Ian, oh, Ian.' Jennie collapsed on to the settee, laughing. 'Aren't you going a bit too fast?'

He looked at her with doubts about her laughter and there was anxiety in his face.

'Don't you want to marry me, Jennie?' Then he, too, laughed. 'Oh, I see what you mean! I've got it the wrong way round. I'm not good at romance, Jennie. Do you love me, for I love you very much and want to marry you more than anything.'

'Oh, Ian, I can't believe it. I've been so miserable all this week and decided the only thing to do was to go back to Edinburgh. We were so close at the week-end and then it all seemed to fall apart.'

He sat by her side, both arms around her.

'I didn't want to rush you, Jennie. You had gone through so much, first with Stuart and then with Adrian. I thought I ought to give you time to catch your breath.' He kissed her tenderly and gently.

'I thought you didn't love me, Ian.'

'I think I've loved you since you were the little McLeod girl,' he said softly.

Jennie had to laugh. 'Oh, Ian, and I hated you.'

'And do you hate me now?'

'No,' she whispered. 'I love you. I love you very much.'